The Blue Camaro

The Blue Camaro

R.P. MacIntyre

For Anjana,
Great name! All
the Best
[signature]
Oct '94

Thistledown Press Ltd.

Canadian Cataloguing in Publication Data

MacIntyre, Rod, 1947-

 The blue Camaro
  ISBN 1-895449-23-5
I. Title.

PS8575.I67B4 1994   jC813'.54 C94-920069-7
PZ7.M327B1 1994

Book design by A.M. Forrie
Cover design by Sean Francis Martin
Typeset in 11pt. New Baskerville by Thistledown Press Ltd.

Printed and bound in Canada by
Hignell Printing Ltd.
Winnipeg, Manitoba

Thistledown Press Ltd.
633 Main Street
Saskatoon, Saskatchewan
S7H 0J8

This book has been published with the assistance of The Canada Council and
the Saskatchewan Arts Board.

For my grandson, Jesse.
And his great grandparents.
For their inspiration and support.

Contents

The Rink

The trouble with being an older brother is you've got to drag your younger brother everywhere you go. That and keep him covered in band-aids any time he scrapes himself, which is about every ten seconds. He's got this thing about his blood leaking out. "I'm leaking!" he says, "I'm leaking!" whenever he cuts himself. He loves band-aids.

So just when stuff starts getting exciting, and you're with your friends, there he is, twenty steps behind you yelling, "Hey! Wait for me!" That's the way it usually is.

It's a couple of years ago on Halloween and as per usual, I'm taking my five year old brother Cory trick-or-treating, but on the way home, we run into some of my friends.

Shane, who is a kind of leader of our gang, has a neat idea. He also has a pellet gun. He says he found it, but with Shane you never know. Anyway, he wants to go over to old man Givens' house and maybe pop out a few windows.

Old man Givens was the principal at our school till he retired last year. Givens the Geezer we called him because of his bony, bald head. And his eyes would burn you like a cigarette. I never actually saw him give the strap because they don't allow that any more, but they said he used to use half a metre of a special thick black licorice because it didn't leave any marks. And then he'd sort of eat it on the school grounds, in front of everybody. He never used to yell. He didn't need to. All he did was whisper and everyone listened.

So anyway, I really want to go with Shane and the gang but Cory is with me, and everything I do when Cory is around, my mom finds out about. I mean Cory is basically a nice kid but he has a mouth as big as a bathtub. So I send him home and promise that if he says a word to Mom, I'll eat all his Halloween candy.

We go over to Givens the Geezer's house and park ourselves behind some bushes. Cam and Jerry have two bars of soap and work over Geezer's car. We try not to laugh too loud. Donny, another friend, has a dozen eggs. He gives a couple to me. We time it so that as Shane shoots his gun, Donny and I fire the eggs through the broken window.

On the count of three we do it, and it works like crazy! Shane's gun doesn't actually make a hole big enough for the eggs to go through. They slobber all over the window instead and it's really just as good. We run like mad! We can hear alarms going off.

It's not even an hour later when I get home. But I hardly walk through the door and I can tell that Bathtub Mouth has said something to Mom and Dad. I look at him and he says, "I told them you were going to take my candy if I said."

Cory gets the candy. I get in trouble, big time.

***

When it's all over, the police find that Shane's gun is hotter than a pancake and he actually goes to Wilbur Hall, a place for jaydees. The rest of us are on some kind of probation where we have to work for people, doing odd jobs.

Guess where I have to work? You got it — Geezer Givens'.

I have to work for three hours a week for ten weeks, just about till Christmas. The kind of stuff I have to do is help him clean the attic, the garage, shovel his walks and a bunch of other odd jobs no one would ever normally do, like washing the basement ceiling.

I guess I deserve every minute of it, but to tell you the truth, it's not as bad as I thought it would be. He taught science at school and is a real electronics nut. He has all these gadgets and doodads, remote this and automatic that, half of which don't work, but of course he's trying to fix.

So far the strangest thing I help him with is this intercom he has hooked up from his house to the garage. He wants to see if it's working. He says it's to hear the garage door opening. Why doesn't he just *look*? Anyway, it works.

I've been there three or four weeks and I've been in every room in his house, except one. This one has its door closed all the time. Then, one day, I find out something I wish I didn't know.

"Come here, Jason," he says.

"Yeah?"

He opens the door and says, "I've been putting this off for months. I guess I should clean it up." In the room is all sorts of sewing stuff, pictures on the walls that look hand-painted, and knickknacks, the kind your grandmother has. It's quite a mess. "My wife's," he says.

"I didn't know you were married." You never think of your bald ex-principal as being married.

"She passed away in August," he says. "My boy wanted to clean it after the funeral, but I wouldn't let him."

"I didn't know you had kids." I can be pretty stupid some times.

He takes a photograph that's above the sewing machine. It's got a man and a woman and a little baby in it. The man is holding the baby.

"This is my boy, Michael. Lives in Toronto. That's my grandson, Bradley. He's six now. And that's Judy," he says, pointing at the picture. "They're coming for Christmas. I'll need the room."

He gives me a package of garbage bags and says, "Put as much of this in these as you can." I notice his hand is shaking. "Take them out to the garage."

He turns and walks away. Fast.

***

The next week it has definitely turned colder and the first mat of snow hides the frozen dirt. You know what I mean — where you kick a lump you think is snow but you just about break your foot.

Anyway, Mr. Givens and I are in the backyard where his garden used to be. There's still dangly frozen tomato plants sticking up and other stuff he wants cleared out. He paces off a square in the snow and says, "Get this as level and clean as you can. This is where it's going."

"What?" I ask.

"The rink," he says. "For my grandson, for Christmas."

I never made a rink before, so I get kind of excited about it and I tell Mom and Dad. Cory, who is big into hockey, thinks this is the cat's meow. He's never seen anyone make a rink before and wants to come and watch. I figure it's not going to hurt anyone, so in a couple of days I take him along to Mr. Givens'.

Cory is sporting two band-aids that cover a rug burn on his chin. He got it diving after an imaginary puck in the living room. He doesn't *need* two band-aids, but that's what he's got.

Mr. Givens is kind of surprised to see me and Cory because I'm not *supposed* to be there for another four days. But I tell him my little brother wants to watch us make the rink and he gets all cheerful and even though he's in the middle of watching a hockey game on TV, he gets dressed, hauls the hose outside and we start putting water where the rink will be.

Mr. Givens has already put little boards around it and in a few minutes, after the water has soaked through the snow, it looks like a box of ugly cold slushy mud. I personally don't see how this is going to be a rink of any kind, but Cory likes the steam going up and chirps at Mr. Givens, asking a zillion questions, like little kids do. Bathtub Mouth.

"Can I skate on it?" asks Cory. He's picking at the top band-aid on his chin.

"Sure you can," says Mr. Givens, "but the first one to skate is going to be my grandson, Brad. You'll like him. He's just about your age."

"When's he coming?" asks Cory.

"He'll be here for Christmas," says Mr. Givens.

"That's a long time," says Cory.

"Not as long as you think," says Mr. Givens. "Well, that should do her for now. All we can do is seal it tonight."

"What's sealing?" asks Cory.

"To keep the water from leaking out. Like a band-aid stops bleeding," says Mr. Givens, smoothing out the one on Cory's chin.

The questions go on and on, while we put the hose away, while Mr. Givens gives us hot chocolate, in fact until we leave.

When we get out of the house and are on our way home, Cory is as quiet as he was noisy at Mr. Givens'. Too quiet.

"What's the matter?" I ask.

"Is sealing really like a band-aid to stop bleeding?"

That's what he asks me, honest. Kids.

***

Over the next few weeks Cory and I go over to Mr. Givens' a lot. Sometimes I pull him over in the sleigh when the snow is fresh, before people get their walks cleared. It's fun. But when the walks are cleared, we walk. It's only a couple of blocks.

The rink actually starts looking like a rink the closer we get to Christmas, and we're actually starting to be friends, especially Mr. Givens and Cory. But the closer Christmas comes, the more edgy Mr. Givens gets. Even Cory notices it. And being Bathtub Mouth, he asks.

"What's the matter, Mr. Givens?"

Mr. Givens is incredibly patient with Cory's questions. He always answers. It would drive me nuts.

"Well, this is the first Christmas without Mrs. Givens, Cory. It just makes me a little sad, that's all."

"Oh," says Cory. He thinks about it for a second, then asks, "Why does that make you sad?"

I can't believe he asks that! That is not the kind of question you ask somebody and expect an answer. It's too personal. But, you guessed it, Mr. Givens answers.

"Well, my son and I tend to argue a bit, and Mrs. Givens was always there to . . . " He looks for words. "To keep us from hurting each other too badly. To stop the bleeding."

"Like a band-aid," says Cory.

"That's right," chuckles Mr. Givens, "Mrs. Givens was like a band-aid."

"She'd seal things."

"She sure would."

When we get outside, I give Bathtub Mouth heck for getting so personal.

"Don't call me Bathtub Mouth," he says.

"Well then don't ask such stupid questions."

"If I don't ask, how am I going to know?" says Cory.

I've got to admit, for a question, it's a pretty good answer. It shuts me up anyway. It also makes me forget the sleigh.

***

Neither of us remember the sleigh till a couple days later when it snows again. Christmas holidays have started and we trudge through the snow, past all the lit houses till we get to Mr. Givens'. Our plan is to scrape the rink and give it one more flood before Mr. Givens' grandson arrives.

But when we get there, the house is dark. It's like a black hole in the block, next to all the other houses. Our sleigh is nowhere in sight. Mr. Givens must have put it in the garage, or maybe behind the house.

We walk around to the back and there is no sled, but the rink is freshly scraped and flooded. The moonlight shines off it like a knife. It's almost spooky, as if something's dead. Cory wants to slide on it, but I say, "No. It's for his grandson first."

We get half a block away when a car pulls into Mr. Givens' driveway. It's them, Mr. Givens, his son and family. They get out of the car. In the clear air we can hear them like they're next to us and Mr. Givens says, "Watch this!" He waves his arms and all of a sudden, his house lights up like a Christmas tree. Spelled out in letters of light is "Welcome Judy, Michael and Brad!! Merry Christmas."

"Oh that's sweet," says a woman I guess is Judy.

"Very nice, Dad," says Michael.

"Can we go in?" says grandson Bradley. "I'm cold."

Cory wants to go back and get the sleigh. But I tell him we should wait till tomorrow.

***

It's Christmas Eve. Cory and I trek over to Mr. Givens'. We go to the door. I'm just about to push the doorbell, when

I stop. I can hear yelling in the house. I look at Cory. He can hear it too.

Sometimes with your brother, you know exactly what each other is thinking, and right now we're both thinking about what Mr. Givens said, about his wife not being there. And how she stopped the fighting.

I turn to go but Cory pushes the doorbell. The yelling stops. Mr. Givens answers the door.

"What do you want?" he says. His face is red.

"Our sleigh," I manage to say.

"In the garage," he says, and closes the door.

A second later we hear the garage door rumble open. We go in and there, leaning up against the far wall, is the sleigh. Right next to it is the intercom I helped test weeks ago. I know it works. Cory looks at me with question marks in his eyes. I turn it on. We listen.

"I don't care if you flooded from here to Calgary . . . " Michael.

"I don't want to go skating. I hate it outside." Brad.

"If Brad doesn't want to go skating, he doesn't have to go skating!" Michael.

"Fine, get the hell out then!" Mr. Givens.

We hear a door slam and through the window we see Mr. Givens heading towards the garage. Cory and I dive behind the car.

"Where's he going?" Judy says over the intercom.

"I don't know." Michael.

"Can't you two get along?" Judy.

Mr. Givens is in the garage by now, with no coat. He doesn't see us.

"Shut up!" he yells at the intercom. It goes silent.

He goes to the wood stacked against the wall. He picks up an axe. Cory and I freeze, if you can freeze even more when you're already frozen.

He leaves the garage, but instead of heading back to the house, he goes to the back yard. Cory runs after him. "Mr. Givens!" he's saying, "Mr. Givens!" I follow Cory.

Mr. Givens is at the rink. He's chopping at it with the ax. He is like a madman. Chips of ice are flying everywhere, splinters of board.

"Mr. Givens, don't!" Cory is yelling. "Mr. Givens!"

Mr. Givens stops. He is sweating and breathing hard.

"Why are you doing that to the ice?" asks Cory.

By now Mr. Givens' son Michael is there, so is Judy his wife.

"Dad stop, come on in," Michael says. He tries to take the axe.

"Leave me alone," says Mr. Givens.

"Are you looking for the seal, Mr. Givens? Remember the first night when we sealed it?" asks Cory.

Mr. Givens' hand relaxes, the axe falls. His eyes turn to Cory. Then he crumbles to the ice with his hands over his face. He starts crying like a baby. "Yes, yes," he says, "I'm looking for the seal."

"What's he talking about? Dad, what are you talking about? Are you okay?" asks Michael. He puts his hand on his father's back.

"He misses your Mom," Cory says. "You shouldn't fight on Christmas."

Silence follows. Like after a tree snap when it's thirty below.

"I'm sorry Dad. I miss her too," says Michael the son. He crouches down beside Mr. Givens and looks for the right words.

"It's a beautiful rink, Dad. I just can't make Brad skate on it. He's not me. When you made all those rinks for me, those were the best days of our lives."

Mr. Givens lifts his head. He straightens up, still on his knees, on the ice.

"Then I got too big for it," continues Michael, "And we didn't play anymore. We needed Mom — we *used* Mom to keep us from fighting. We got to learn to do it alone, Dad."

Mr. Givens looks up at the stars, then at his son.

"I love you Dad," says Michael. And they hug. Right there on the rink.

We all stand there, like icicles broken from the eaves. We look at each other, and then away, not knowing what to say.

Except for Cory. He asks, "Can I skate on the rink now, Mr. Givens?"

Mr. Givens smiles through his tears. "It's all yours," he says.

"Well, yours too," says Cory.

"Maybe Brad will come out when he sees you skating," says Michael.

"We'll fix the holes though," says Cory.

"Yes we will," says Mr. Givens.

He's a neat kid, Cory. I decide then and there I won't call him Bathtub Mouth anymore.

Soon after, we wish them a Merry Christmas and head home. We forget the sleigh again, but it doesn't matter. We'll be back.

━━O━━   Mary

Our summers here burn the flat landscape brittle and turn living things to yellow ash and stone, while a scant three months later the same white sun fixes everything into ice. Things are violently the same. Only the season differs. This is the prairies. We learn to live with extremes that cannot be explained.

This is why the prairie sky is so full of ghosts.

Every now and then some event so weird occurs, so inexplicably and unimaginably weird, that you are sure it *cannot have happened.* Yet that event is somehow carved so deeply with living chisels into that place in your mind called memory that you know it has happened, absolutely, just as summer follows winter.

I have this memory of when I was young, very young — I couldn't have been much more than two. The reason I know I am that age is because I am lying in my crib in my parent's bedroom. Everything in this memory is complete, the walls, the crib, the little white jail bars, the dangling mobile above me — everything. But, I know it can't have happened because included in the picture are two people making my parent's bed. They are both my mother. I look at one and then the other. It's like a little movie, and this is what I see.

The two of them shoo the cat off the bed, not in mirrored synchronism, but separately. One stands and says the word "shoo," the other bends and flicks her wrist at the cat who hisses and walks away. Then they spread a sheet and I can feel the breeze the sheet makes as they hold it high then luff it down onto the bed and pull it tight. They fluff the pillows and cover it all with a rose-coloured bed spread. The cat jumps back onto the bed. Then both these people smile alternately at me. The pair disappear. The memory fades.

I have two mothers, in my memory, who made that bed, who look like twins. A matching pair.

This puzzles me. Even in my memory I am puzzled while it is happening. I know that something is definitely wrong with this memory. So two years ago, when my aunt died, Mom's older sister, I try to make the memory real. I ask my mother if she ever had a twin.

All she does is laugh, "Whatever made you ask that?"

I don't know how to tell her.

***

When I was born they called me Mary, after my great, great grandmother, Mary McGinnis. No one else in the family seems to be named after an ancient dead relative, so I don't quite understand why I should be. Mary: drab, boring, and plain. From Cape Breton Island, Nova Scotia, Canada.

My mother was a McGinnis, Angela McGinnis. When she married my dad, she took his name, Flegal. Angela Flegal. Dad is from Saskatchewan, which makes me Mary Flegal. The prairies match my name: drab, boring, plain.

These are the essentials of my family history, except for the ghosts.

The cat in the memory, or dream, or whatever, is Silvie.

Last year, it was obvious — Silvie was getting old. Her fur looked fake. And for a cat, nineteen is old, as old as me.

If cats have nine lives, then Silvie had used up at least eight. She was hanging on by a whisker, a broken whisker. They used to be long and dignified. They balanced her head and made her look like a tight rope walker. But she had only a sad few left that were broken and bent. I think she was going blind too. She walked into walls. Maybe she was practising to be a ghost.

When I was younger I was afraid of such things, but I guess they were mostly conjurings of my imagination. I would hide beneath the covers convinced that some thing could reach out from under the bed with gnarled, cold and scaly fingers, grab me and take me forever into unspeakable darkness. It never did, of course, because I would leave a light on and Silvie would join me in bed.

The thing about Silvie is that she could see ghosts. She would be mid-stride walking across a room, when all of a sudden she would freeze. She would arch her back, spit at some invisible thing, watch it till it was apparently gone, then continue her way as though nothing had happened. She was used to it. They were common in her lives. In mine, they are rare.

***

Two weeks after Granddad McGinnis retired, grandma had a heart attack and died. Granddad lasted two more months, then he too was gone. This left Aunt Dolores as my mother's closest family. I used to tease her that she was my favourite aunt, as in, "How did my favourite aunt mess up today?" Or, "When's my favourite aunt going to quit smoking?" And she would always answer, "Ask me no questions, I'll tell you no lies."

When Mom and I were fighting, which was as often as not, Aunt Dolores would come between us always and mediate some kind of peace.

"She's the only mom you've got," she would say, "and I'm your only aunt." Technically this was not true. My dad's brothers are married, but they are not McGinnises, and when Aunt Dolores said she was my only aunt, she was just affirming the surviving sisterhood of the McGinnises, and that we three shared something special together. However, I'm sure that even if I had a half-dozen McGinnis aunts, Aunt Dolores would have been my favourite.

She had a tiny perfect body, and wore only jeans with sweaters that bagged aimlessly about her like the loose quilting of a tick. Yet it would look as though it was tailored for her and she would carry herself like a bushy-tailed cat.

She always gave me books to read, books by people I had never heard of. She specialized in obscurity. She herself was an artist, but had little to show for it because of what she did for a living — picture framing, for other artists. Her own drawings were of women, faceless charcoals that always left you feeling that you were looking at something you were not supposed to see, a feeling of regret. Which was quite ironic, because you never met a less penitent person than Aunt Dolores. Her face was always open and smiling.

Then, when I was sixteen, busy with my hormones and boys trying to grope my breasts, Aunt Dolores got a lump in hers. Inside that perfectly disguised body. She refused any treatment. I don't know why. She grew so small before she died that I knew what she looked like when she was a little girl. A little girl and an old woman. She was forty-five.

***

In the summer we always go to the lake, to my grand-parents' cabin, the Flegals. We pack up our camper, Mother, Dad, and I, put Silvie in her cage and head north. For one weekend the whole family gathers — everyone, all my uncles, aunts and cousins. Then everyone, all my uncles, aunts and cousins remember why we only do it once a year. At least one of my little cousins has to go the hospital with a cut or broken bone, and at least one of my uncles gets too drunk or fights with another of my uncles. And Gramma always catches the most fish or the biggest fish, and Grandpa always pouts or blames and makes excuses.

But last summer was the first summer without Aunt Dolores.

It was one of those days when everyone was out, either fishing or golfing or at the beach. It was a languorous, quiet day. You could not have cut a more perfect day from the eye of summer. Even the insects were still. A perfect day for sulking in the shade. My mother would not let me have the car and I was at the cabin, alone, reading. Just me and Silvie.

Now you've got to know this about Silvie. Old and reliable though she was, and as long as she'd been around, she had never shown affection. Never. She was like Gramma Flegal that way — you know she loves you, but she would never show it.

At any rate, I was sitting at the picnic table on the back deck with one of the books from Aunt Dolores that I was only then getting around to reading. Silvie was across from me, curled in her favourite spot taking in the good lake air or whatever it is cats do when they are in their favourite spots seeming to be at peace with themselves. I suddenly was filled with a very strange feeling. It's a feeling that Aunt Dolores was there, there at the cabin.

I looked up from my book and the feeling was so strong that I actually called, quietly, "Aunt Dolores?"

At the sound of my voice, Silvie rose from her perch, and sat, her eyes suddenly alert. I was absolutely certain that my aunt was near.

"Aunt Dolores?" I struggled to think of something to say. So I said the first thing that came to mind. "*Ask me no questions, I'll tell you no lies.*"

Precisely at that moment, Silvie jumped down from her perch, strode solemnly across the deck, jumped up on the picnic table, strolled over and kissed my nose. And just to make sure I didn't miss what she had done, she kissed me again. Something she had never in her life done before.

I knew that Aunt Dolores was there. I thanked her for the book. I told her I missed her. A sudden breeze kicked up the leaves on the trees. Then, just as quickly as the Aunt Dolores feeling came, it left. And so did Silvie. Back to her perch.

I didn't tell anyone.

***

It's the sad truth that Silvie was not only going blind, she was going deaf too. For some stupid reason, she wandered out onto the middle of the street and parked herself there. She could not have heard the car coming or she would have moved. But she didn't. Stupid cat. I'll miss her.

***

It's a month after the family lake scene and a week since Silvie's passing. The house is still covered in cat hair. Mother is not a good housekeeper. It doesn't matter. In a few weeks I'll be going away to school, to university. There I will study creative writing. It's something I have a flair for, though my teacher sometimes says that I am given to certain excesses when I try too hard. I'm glad the course is not offered here. It will get me away from home.

So this is the last vacation I will take with my parents. I feel I owe it to them, since they are paying my way to school. This year's destination is my mother's ancestral home, where the McGinnises settled in the new world, Cape Breton, to a tiny hamlet called East Bay. We have some ancient relative who supposedly survives there, an uncle or great uncle, Allistair McGinnis. He used to be a miner, my grandfather's only contact with his birth place, a man with whom he had occasionally been in touch before he died. Mother's mission is to find this man. Dad's is to golf.

I have never been to Nova Scotia before, never east of Toronto. I have only a vague idea of what to expect. I somehow have this image that it is wet, rainy and grey, that gulls will sweep eternally over an eternal coast.

We land in Halifax and rent a car. Part of my image is correct. It is wet, rainy and grey. But no gulls and no coast. The first thing I notice is that rain does not fall, vertically, as it does on the prairies. It blows directly at you, horizontally. It's as though gravity is confused. Dad is annoyed. This is lousy weather to golf in.

But soon enough we approach the Canso Causeway, the hand-built link of land between the Isle of Cape Breton and the rest of North America. It is only now that I see a coast, replete with gulls and fishing boats. And as we drive across the Causeway, the horizontal rain fades to a drizzle and suddenly, like a great welcoming ribbon looped about a giant gift, a rainbow strikes against the sky above the green rolling hills of Cape Breton itself.

"Wow," says Mother.

"Wow," says Dad.

"Wow," says I. We're dumbstruck. Words are useless.

***

It is the next morning and we are at a small motel near Sydney. It seemed as though we would never arrive, stopping every twenty minutes or so to gape and gawk at something even more wonderful than our last stop twenty minutes before, at an endless procession of hills, valleys, speckled farms and mighty north Atlantic waves genuflecting up against rocks the size of churches. But now we are here.

After we deposit Dad and his clubs at his idea of some green heaven, Mother and I are on our own. We have never travelled together, just the two of us, and it feels, suddenly, as though we do not have a past. That there is only this present, this strange place, where we travel together as equals, performing a simple direct task: to find Allistair McGinnis. But it is a silly task. We do not know where this man lives. Or if he is alive. Yet we strike out for the only road to a dot on the map, to this place, East Bay.

We have turned off the main highway and are snaking our way through highland fields where a forest once grew. And is trying once again to grow. The fields are filling back in with scrub spruce or fir — "Christmas trees" is what we'd call them on the prairies. What open fields there are, seem shallow and butt up against sheer walls of rock or steeply banked woods.

Every few hundred yards there is a farm house or shack and a lane marked with a mailbox turning up towards a scruffy yard with dead machines and a clutter of weather-beaten buildings. We are looking at the mailboxes, trying to read the scuffed names. There are Rankins, Rosses, Campbells, Poiriers, Purdys and an endless array of Mc's and Mac's.

Mother pulls the car tight to a mailbox whose name we can't make out. A derelict truck sits rusting on its frame near the gate and weeds grow tall in the lane. At the end of the lane is a two-part structure that may have once been a large, proper house with an add-on kitchen. It looks abandoned, collapsing from the middle into its foundation. But the add-on, attached to the main structure, is somehow independently firm, its paint less weathered than the rest. A stove pipe sticks out from a windowpane, drifting smoke.

"Want to check?" asks Mother. She turns the ignition off.

I don't think she is asking me to wander up alone. She is merely seeking consensus. Though there is no way of identifying that we've found the right place, we know we have. And the question is, really, do we want to meet this ghost?

We do.

Leaving the car by the gate, we walk past the rotting truck and through the tall pale grass of late summer. We approach a small wooden landing that buckles in front of a screen door. Next to the door, on the landing, sits a battered chrome chair. Dirty white stuffing swells from the split vinyl on its back and a large tabby cat lies curled on its seat. The cat hears us, jerks up its head, and in two swift kicks disappears beneath the landing.

I feel Mother's fingers brush the back of my hand. I glance at her. She's staring straight ahead at the tattered screen door. I look too.

Behind the screen a tall shadow shifts. It is the shadow of a man. He reaches forward and as he pushes open the door. The shadow peels from him and he is fully awash in sunlight. He wears no shoes, but stands in grey woollen socks. A pair of dirty green work pants hang loosely on him, notched at the waist by a large brass belt buckle. A shrunken grey woollen sweater covers his torso. His face is fissured with time and pale as the dying grass behind us.

But his eyes. His eyes are green as spring. And unblinking, he fixes them on Mother's. They stand, locked in time, and for a brief, imperceptible second all the fissures vanish from his face.

"Mary?" he asks, still looking into my mother's eyes. "Mary ... McGinnis," he says.

"No," says my mother, "That's Mary." She glances at me. "My name is Angela."

"Wee Mary," says the old man, still looking at my mother. But now he is confused.

"Angela Flegal," says my mother. "I was a McGinnis. Mary was named after her great, great grandmother." She slides her hand under my arm.

The old man looks at me. He cocks his head slightly, and says, "Angela. You were a wee thing too."

"We're from Saskatchewan," says Mother. "Are you Allistair McGinnis?"

"Allistair." The old man straightens. He smiles. "Allistair's been dead for twenty years," he says. "I was thinking of him today." He considers us for a moment, two strangers from the present. "Would you like to come in for some tea?" he asks.

We do.

He tells us his name is Alexander, Alexander John McGinnis. He is eighty-eight years old. He remembers well my mother's grandmother, and is amazed at their resemblance. I am my own great aunt in likeness. Angela McKay, one we never knew existed. He tells us where they lived and how their men piped in the hills, cut wood, or mined in the deep dark mines. How the women died in childbirth or consumption, or left to travel West, never to be heard from again. It is an uncanny visit to the past.

On the way back to the golf course to pick up Dad, we know that he has missed some inarticulate thing, and that we will try to tell him about it, but we will fail.

I tell my mother of her double. I tell her about the lake and Silvie with Dolores.

Sitting beside me, driving the rented car with her eyes fixed on the road, I see my mother's ghost and my mother's ghost is me.

Eat, Sleep, Jump High for Smarties

Kathy had this little dog, a miniature poodle whose name was Tupper. Normally I hate little dogs. They're constantly yapping and they bounce around like there's a tiny invisible trampoline under them all the time. But I didn't mind Tupper.

He was reasonably calm and quiet and was very business-like. He wore a little gray suit and you could almost imagine him carrying a brief case. Except he was a junkie. He would do anything for a piece of chocolate. He would spring five feet straight up and snap a Smartie out of the air like it was a frisbee. Kathy said he reminded her of me, totally dedicated to money. I wish life was that simple — eat, sleep, and jump-high-for-Smarties. Except it isn't.

I like money. Lots of it. Wads of it, bursting from my wallet. Money is good. I never have enough.

I like money so much, I'm even willing to work for it.

The first job I ever had was selling cool-aid, "Randy's Cool-Aid, 25 Cents a Glass." I set up my stand in some bushes

behind the ninth hole on the golf course across the street. I
was six years old. Business was so good, I decided to franchise.
I set up stands on the sixth and twelfth holes too. I got my
friends to run them. Then it rained for a week and I lost my
business partners. On top of that, some big kids came and
robbed me. I got out of the cool-aid business. It taught me an
important lesson: there are things you just can't control.

By the time I was fourteen, I had two paper routes plus a
lawn care business that netted me five grand a year. That's
right, folks — five G's.

So last year, for my sixteenth birthday, I bought myself a
new set of wheels. My folks, in a mindless fit of generosity,
sprang for half the insurance which cost almost as much as
the car. Well, it's not exactly a car and it's not exactly new. It's
a Jeep 4X4. It's only seven years old, and in great shape. I got
a trailer to go with it, so I can tow my mower in summer and
snowblower in winter. Business has been good.

In the summer I put extra fertilizer on people's lawns and
water them more so I'll have to cut them more often, and in
winter I pray for those Arctic highs and B.C. lows to mix and
make lots of snow. This disgusts Kathy. However, she likes the
portable CD player I got her for her birthday.

I'm also working as a packer at Super Store, (a.k.a. Stupor
Store), for fifteen hours a week which brings me to problem
one: school is beginning to interfere with work. I mean, what
does school teach you about making money? Especially
classes like English.

Which brings me to problem two: Kathy. Kathy Stetson.
Kathy's in my Biology class. And Language Arts. She writes
poetry and stuff and gets it published in the school paper. It's

always about death and war and other heavy topics. It doesn't rhyme, so I don't know how good it is.

I don't *want* to like Kathy, but I do. She wears black all the time, even though it's no longer cool. She's forever burying her nose in some kind of book, except when she's looking at you. When she does that, she has this little sneer on her lips, like there's something about you she finds *very* funny. She drives me crazy. So the first time I asked her out she said, "What took you so long?" She has this knack of making you feel like an idiot and like a genius at the same time. Women.

Kathy has this twisted view of the universe. She thinks that money is evil and that everybody should throw their cash into a great big pot and take what they need. She figures if everybody did that, there'd be enough to feed everyone on the planet. I suppose it's a good idea if all you want to do is eat, but I want to know where they're going to keep the pot and who's going to be the first to throw their money in.

Kathy also thinks you go to school for an "education," that you don't go for the piece of paper — diploma or degree — which makes you worth something in the market place. My argument is that an education is just fine, but you got to learn something. Something useful, not how a pig fetus gets rid of its waste products, like what we took yesterday in Biology class. I mean, what good, in everyday life, is knowing how a pig works? Zip. Nothing, as near as I can figure out. That doesn't stop Kathy though. She slashes away at pickled meat like some kind of demented butcher.

***

Mr. Hawes is our English teacher. He does his best to make it interesting for us. He cracks bad jokes, wears funny ties and encourages us to be creative. He is also quite short. So when he wants to make a big point, he'll stand on the waste basket. When he wants to make a bigger point, he'll stand on his chair. When he wants to make a *really* big point, he'll stand on his desk. Today he was practically hanging off the ceiling.

"Don't you guys *know* what a metaphor is?!" he screams at us. "Is it so *hard* to under*stand* what a *metaphor* is?" He is teetering from the edge of his desk. "We spend three days talking about it and you still don't *know what a metaphor is?*" The little vein in his forehead is pulsing purple. He's going to croak right in front of us, topple off the desk and die. And we will have killed him.

What has got him to this point is our stupidity.

Our class isn't big. There's twenty-five of us and we sit in four rows. I'm the third person in the third row. He started at the top of the first row reading the first person's attempt at writing a metaphor.

"This isn't a metaphor" he says, after reading it aloud. It was something about chickens. How they cluck.

The next one he reads is about trees. *The trees blow in the breeze, they bend, they bow.* "Trees *do* that, give me something they *don't* do."

Then someone's cat. *The cat springs like its leg is full of muscle.* Not a metaphor.

Then about a car. *It races, like a well-oiled machine.* "It *is* a well-oiled machine."

Then a rainbow, *shining high in the sky, like a big bow.* "It *is* a big bow."

He reads them, and after each one he reads, he gets madder. "Can't anybody in this room write a metaphor?"

The truth is that nobody can. Certainly not me. But not even Kathy. I feel sorry for Kathy. She writes a whole story.

It's about this guy who has an apple tree. And he collects all the apples, then eats as many of them as he can. But he's tired after all this eating and picking, so he wants to take a nap. But he's afraid that someone will come along and take his apples while he's sleeping. So he pees on them.

When he awakes from his nap, he's hungry. But he can't tell the difference between what's been peed on and what hasn't. So he ends up eating all his apples trying to find one that's clean.

Mr. Hawes reads this and the whole class laughs.

Mr. Hawes does not. "What's so funny?" he asks. He asks it in such a way that everyone shuts up. He looks around the room. It's so quiet you could hear a bird fart.

"It's not a metaphor."

"Yes it is," blurts Kathy.

Mr. Hawes arches his eyebrows, like this somehow makes him taller. "For what?" he asks.

"For *Life*," says Kathy.

Mr. Hawes' eyebrows sink to the middle of his nose. "Maybe it's a metaphor for *your* life, Ms Stetson . . . "

"A friend of mine," she interrupts. She doesn't exactly look at me, but I know of whom she is thinking. So does half the class. I hear a few titters. Neither Mr. Hawes nor myself think this is particularly funny.

"Don't interrupt me. If I want interruptions, I'll call for them."

"Then they wouldn't be interruptions," interrupts Kathy, again.

This is when he flies off the handle. He climbs the waste basket and uses words like "attitudes", then the chair, with words like "respect", till finally he is tilting dangerously blue-faced from the desk with something about "thoughts, learning and creativity being the essence of life."

In the meantime, while he is ranting, I am writing, or rather, rewriting. I know that what I wrote in the first place is no better than what anyone else in the class has written. That *the grass grows green as Christmas trees,* is not a metaphor. That if I don't come up with something good, we will either be attending the funeral of Mr. Hawes or he will have a major nervous breakdown and drag an M-16 into the class and fire at us, splattering pieces of our stupid bodies across the blackboard.

But I am hurt, a wounded animal scorned in public by the woman I love, and I am writing now from my soul, passionate and true. I ignore Mr. Hawes as he leaps from his perch and lands two desks in front of me. He reads another failed metaphor. We are one step closer to the M-16. He shreds the offending paper to shrapnel and flings them into the air. I keep on writing.

The bits of paper descend like snow, landing on our heads. The person in front of me has written his doomed metaphor into a notebook. Mr. Hawes rails, and fires it across the room. It splashes against the blackboard and slides dismally onto the floor.

I stop writing.

He snatches my paper from my desk. He snarls: *The grass grows money green and mowed, spits spent clippings at me till I choke for a dollar.*" I have no idea what this means, but it is what I have written.

Mr. Hawes visibly pales, to a more natural colour. He reads it again. Silently. He stops shaking. He clears his throat. "A metaphor," he says, nodding his head.

The class roars approval, but they do it very, very quietly. In fact, you can't hear a thing.

"An image," he says, disbelieving. "This is good," he says. "This is actually quite, good. Thank you, Randy. Randy is the only one in the class who knows what a metaphor is." His voice rises, along with his eyebrows. "*This, ladies and gentlemen, is poetry.* The metaphor for the greenness of the grass, is money. And it is so overpowering, this greenness, in tiny ways, 'spitting clippings', that it chokes the writer. It threatens to kill him in revenge."

I had no idea it could mean all that. He continues talking, but I am not listening. I am trying not to smile. I am glowing inside. I have just done something that no one else in the class has done. *I have written poetry.* I have written words on paper that have power, that have life. That have *saved* lives — ours, and probably Mr. Hawes' too. I have made his day. He is concluding his speech.

"This, Kathy, is what your whole story could have been. But Randy did it in one short line. That's the power of a metaphor." Mr. Hawes is smiling now, happy once again to be a teacher, to awaken our minds, to broaden our horizons.

The only trouble is that Kathy doesn't want her mind broadened at the moment.

"There's no money in it," she says.

"What?" Mr. Hawes doesn't quite believe what he is hearing. Neither do I.

"I said the trouble with poetry is that it doesn't make any money." This sounds like something I would say, in fact, have probably already said.

"Do you mean to say it has no value unless it makes money?" Mr. Hawes asks, eyebrows up.

"No, but some people would say that," and she looks directly at me.

Which makes Mr. Hawes look at me.

Which makes the whole class look at me.

It's like a spell. Twenty-five pairs of eyes cut into me. My soul is bleeding out. They are peering into my measly money-soaked soul. What's the matter? Are they forgetting? *I'm the one who wrote the poetry.* And all of a sudden I get this blinding flash. I look at my bleeding soul lying there on the floor and it has no meaning. All the money in the world stacked up together has no meaning. It's just a stack of money. But words, even two words, have more meaning than all the money in the world. And I know this to be the truth and at the same time I know that all the poetry in the world wouldn't buy you a loaf of bread.

"I don't know what to say," is what I say.

***

I've only been a poet for two days and I've already skipped one day of work. This, I believe, is what a poet would do. I can feel my hair growing longer, my cheeks sinking. I turn my jaundiced eye on everything and sneer. On everything, that is, but Kathy. For Kathy I just want to be a puppy dog. I want to sit on her lap and pant. I will cuddle and look cute. I will be happy there. I will not pee. I promise.

Except that now I'm a poet, Kathy doesn't talk to me. I mean, we go out but she doesn't say anything. She sits there, brooding. She gives one word answers, "Yes," "No," "Maybe." I don't know what to do. If you're not going to talk to someone, what's the point of being with them? And now she's started taking Tupper with her everywhere she goes. She holds the dog on her lap and talks to him. She talks to him. This dog is where I want to be. I am beginning to hate Tupper.

I am driving down 8th Street with Kathy and Tupper. It is snowing. I am thinking, *snow, I hate snow. I will have to start my snowblower. But it is soft snow. The snow is like burnt clouds. Hot snow.* This is when I realize I am doomed. That if I am driving down 8th Street in my Jeep with my girlfriend and her businessman dog, neither of who are talking to me, and I am thinking thoughts about burning clouds and hot snow, that there is no hope for me. That I probably really am a poet and that I will write great poetry that no one will read till I am dead. That I will live a totally useless but meaningful life.

I unwrap a chocolate bar, steering for a moment with my elbows. Tupper perks up. Kathy looks straight ahead. I take a bite of the bar. It's an O Henry. The system I have is to suck the chocolate, chew the peanuts, then get down to the fudgey centre. It lasts longer that way. I flip a chocolate crumb to Tupper. He snaps it out of the air.

"Don't," says Kathy.

I break off another crumb and do it again. Tupper is pleased.

"Don't," says Kathy, again.

I break off another piece, but before I do anything with it, Kathy grabs the whole bar from my hand and in one motion lowers her window and flings the O Henry into the night.

Tupper follows it, hurling himself out the window.

***

I don't know if you've ever tried to hold a pet doggy funeral in the middle of winter, but there are certain problems. Problem one: digging a hole. Problems two to ten: consoling the pet doggy's owner.

In Kathy's backyard the snow was deep and I cleared a plot of ground about two metres square. Into the centre I threw a plastic bag of leaves left over from the fall, soaked it with charcoal lighter fluid and set it ablaze. This was to thaw the ground, though for a moment I thought of cremating the dog. The fire succeeded in turning the top two inches of soil into muck. Beneath that, it was still frozen hard as rock.

Kathy was in tears. Tupper's stiff little body would not be covered by two inches of mud. What did the poet do? He borrowed Kathy's dad's drill, fitted it with an extension, knelt on his knees and drilled into the frozen ground, chewing it up as best he could. Then he shoveled and hacked with an axe till there was a hole deep enough to fit the doggy's corpse. In it he first placed a box of Smarties, then lowered the dog on top.

Kathy could not look as the poet scraped the frozen earth back into the hole, covering the little dog.

As I packed the mound with the back of the shovel, an amazing feeling came over me, a feeling that I was burying me, and I could imagine how that shovel must sound if I were under the earth and how final it would be. That there would be no more. That the snow is cold, not hot. That I was burying the poet too. I wanted to dig the dog back up and lay my own head there. I dropped the shovel. I hugged Kathy, in her black coat. We stood there in the frozen snow.

***

We stood there a long time, but it was Kathy who finally said, "Let's go." And we came here, to this muffin shop where we always go for coffee. Some friends join us. Kathy is telling stories of when Tupper was a pup. We are laughing. He once ate the tongue from her father's shoe, then spat it up. Back in the shoe. "He was just putting it where he got it from." Each story she tells is funnier than the last. Yet, while she does this, I am asking her with my eyes or with my mind or some way that I cannot see, *How come you aren't talking to me?* And in among her tales she answers, *Because I am the poet, not you.* There are things you just can't control.

The one story she does not tell is how Tupper would jump high for Smarties.

Doing Something

It's one of those beautiful days. If it was music, it couldn't be metal or rap, it'd be a great ballad with slow clean guitar riffs. The sky is blue, the trees are green and the lake is calm as glass. It's so perfect and beautiful it makes your eyes hurt. It's the perfect day for doing something. The question is, what?

"I don't care what you do," Dad says, getting into the car, "just don't touch the boat."

"But . . . "

"Don't even *think* about it," says Dad.

"And be careful," says Mom. The car rumbles off.

Mom always says that to me, ever since last summer when I broke my knee in Jansen's backyard. This is when I took up guitar. Something to do while I was hobbling around in a cast. The knee's fine now, but every now and then when I'm walking and when I least expect it, it does a vanishing act, just pretends that it's not there, and I wind up on my face. It's embarrassing sometimes but no big deal.

Anyway, everybody else is doing something. Dad and
Mom have gone golfing. My sister, Karen, and her friends are
practising to be movie stars (good luck). My bud, Snake, has
gone north fishing with his Uncle Jack. My other bud, Jodie,
is back in town going to his orthodontist. And I'm stuck here
alone. With nothing to do. I can't even play guitar. It's at the
shop getting fixed. Broken neck.

When I say my sister is practising to be a movie star, I'm
not kidding. She and all her other sixteen year old friends
have all gone gaga over these two dudes who pulled into the
Stones Throw Restaurant and Motel in a black van with
Sunrise Films Inc. written on it. I follow them.

They have sort of long hair and sunglasses. One of them
needs a shave. They immediately started wandering around
looking for "locations", places where the scenery is best and
that sort of thing. That's what they tell me. I tell them that
around here that shouldn't be a problem because most of the
scenery is like out of a movie anyway, except for the dump
and Jansen's back yard.

The other thing they do is put a notice up on the board
outside the Stones Throw Restaurant. It says,

EXTRAS NEEDED
for Television Commercial
Ten females, ages sixteen to twenty.
One male, sixteen to twenty.
Apply in person for audition, Room 16, Stones Throw Motel
Ten A.M. to Two P.M. Tuesday, July 8.
Sunrise Films Inc.

And now everybody wants to be a movie star. Except me. I won't be fifteen till next month.

The two guys disappear into the motel and I wander down to the lake shore just to see if anything's happening and to kind of look at the boat that's been declared out of bounds while Dad's not around. It's a fat fifteen-and-a-half feet, not exactly built for speed, but it goes all right with the ninety horse Merc flat out. I mean, at least it makes waves, and does a pretty good job towing skiers. But not today. There's nobody to ski with anyway. What a waste.

All that's around is a couple of little kids playing in the sand. They don't even look up, they're so into building a sand castle. I almost want to join them. I find a good flat skipper and see how many times I can bounce it on the water. I throw. It hits. Perfect. Fourteen skips! It's got to be a record!

Big deal. There's nobody here to see it. The little kids didn't even notice. I could jump in the lake and drown and nobody would notice.

I cut through the woods to get up to the road, thinking that I might as well go to the Stones Throw. Maybe something is happening there. It's the only place to hang out if you're not at the lake itself.

In the motel parking lot sits the black van with Sunrise Films Inc. on it. As I enter the restaurant, a woman with the clip board smiles at me on her way out. I try to smile back but she is gone before I get a chance. So I'm actually all the way in the restaurant before I notice what I'm in the middle of.

Girls.

There's more girls here than I knew existed, I mean at the lake. I want to say they're every different size and shape, but they're not. They're all the same. The smell of hair spray just about knocks me out. I feel like I'm in the middle of a rock video without the band. All these girls, and every one of them wants to be a movie star. There's two or three guys here too. I guess they're auditioning for the sixteen-year-old-guy part. The girls are looking at me, like, what am I doing here? I've got to get out.

I turn to leave, I take a step, but . . . my knee isn't there!

So I'm laying on the floor. I open my eyes and above me I see a blurry circle of tanned wanna-be-movie-star faces. They're staring at me like I was a car accident, when one of them leans out and says, "Oh, it's Kenny! Are you okay?" It's one of my sister's friends.

"I'm fine," I say, "I'm fine," but on the way down to the floor I guess I banged my head against the counter and I can feel the egg growing. The truth is I'm woozy as heck.

But Karen's friend is helping me to my feet saying, "You're sister's over there. I'll help you." And she does. She half hauls me across the restaurant full of wanna-be-movie-stars to where Karen is sitting with somebody in a booth.

Karen is not wearing her glasses, so she doesn't know it's me — yet. Karen is one of those people who would prefer to squint and be blind than wear her glasses and see.

When she finally recognizes that it is me, she is not pleased. I know what she's thinking. She's thinking I did this all on purpose, just to get some attention, just to wreck her day, her chance to be a movie star. She is giving me one of her Kenny-can't-you-ever-do-anything-right looks.

I sit down next to her, holding the lump on my head with my right hand. I look across the table.

And there she is, the girl of my — okay, I'm not going to say dreams, because not only is it such a cliché, but I've never seen anyone like this before, not even in my — dreams. For all future dreams, this is the face in place. Anyway, the sound you hear is probably my jaw hitting the table.

"What happened?" asks Karen.

I pick up my jaw. "Nothing. I fell." My voice doesn't even crack. Victory! A small one, I admit. I wipe the drool from my chin.

In the middle of all these wanna-be-movie-stars is a face that could actually be one. A Vision. Her angled features cut the air like drum beats cased in black hair. Her lips are like full long notes on a slide guitar. Her eyes — I can't see her eyes. She's wearing shades.

"Who is this?" asks the perfect Vision across the table.

"Oh," says Karen. "This is my brother Kenny. He's always falling."

"Yeah," I agree like an idiot. "Or slipping. I slip a lot too." Something I'm doing right now.

"Oh, I'm Cynthia," says Cynthia the Vision. "How are you?"

She presents her perfect hand across the table. She wants me to shake it. I can't believe this. *None* of Karen's friends ever want to talk to me much less touch me, willingly, with their hands. If I were a puppy dog, I'd be peeing on the floor right about now. But I'm not and I don't. Instead, I reach for her hand as calmly as I can. I grasp it, gently, trying not to sweat. Her hand is warm and dry. Golden brown. The back of it feels like butterfly wings.

"Fine," I say, but something is wrong. Something is uncomfortable about this hand shake.

"Oh," she says, "the hand of a musician."

Well if I wasn't already a bowl of jelly, I'm right now a pool of goo.

"How did you know?" the goo manages to ask.

"The callouses on your fingers."

I've given her my *left* hand, the wrong hand! The one with leather-tipped fingers from playing guitar. That's what's wrong with this handshake! My *right* hand is still propping up my stupid head.

"Oh, yeah," I say, recovering my hand from her, "I play guitar. But it's broken."

"Is it two yet?" asks Karen.

Cynthia, hardly looking towards her watch, sort of brushes it with her long fingers. "Five to," she says.

"I've got to go," says Karen. "My audition. How do I look?"

"Fine, I hope," says Cynthia.

"Yeah, why am I asking you?" says Karen. I take this to mean that Karen is admitting she doesn't have much hope in front of the most beautiful girl in the world. "Wish me luck," she adds.

We do. She's going to need all the luck she can get. Squeezing by me, and squinting to see which way the door is, Karen leaves. Me alone. With my tongue in knots. I try not to ogle at Cynthia.

A fly lands on the table in front of us. Something to focus on. It strolls over to a grain of sugar and starts doing something. An hour passes. Maybe two. I've got to untangle my tongue, so I ask a question.

"What do flies do anyway?" I ask as casually as I can.

"I beg your pardon?"

"Oh nothing," I say. I realize that this might be the stupidest question ever asked on the planet earth.

Another hour passes. The fly buzzes off.

"It's a beautiful day," says Cynthia the Vision.

"Yeah, yeah, it's beautiful." I couldn't agree more.

"We should be doing something," says Cynthia the Mind Reader. "I mean on a beautiful day like today."

"Exactly what I was thinking!" I say, practically jumping off the seat.

"Any ideas?" she asks.

"Ideas. I've got tons of ideas," I lie. Now I've got to name one. "Like we could go for a walk or something."

"I don't think so," says Cynthia. Her lips go into a kind of curious pout.

I've got to come up with something big, or I'm going to lose her before she realizes I'm here.

"How about a boat ride? In my boat."

"You have a boat?"

"Well it's not actually mine. It's my dad's. He sort of left me in charge." He did leave me in charge, in charge of not touching it.

"Are you sure you'd like to take me?"

"Sure? Of course I'm sure!" She doesn't know how sure. I'll be grounded for a week, but who cares. This is the chance of a lifetime. A beautiful girl and me, alone, on the boat. If we just happen to run out of gas on the middle of the lake . . .

"Well if you're sure, let's go then."

"Great!" I say, a little too loud. I look around at all the wanna-be-movie-stars. A thought occurs to me.

"But what time is your audition?"

"What audition?" asks Maid Cynthia.

"The one that everybody's going to, that Karen went to."

"I'm not going," says Cynthia.

"No? Why not?"

"I'm blind, Ken, in case you haven't noticed."

I haven't noticed. I haven't noticed anything. She's just been sitting there. For all I know, she doesn't have any legs. I find myself wanting to look underneath the table, to check. I restrain myself. I panic instead. If I have an expression on my face, it's probably one with lots of teeth, a broken smile I'm trying to fix.

"You're blind?"

"I'm blind," says the Vision.

"Oh," I say, seeing now the reason for her sunglasses, the way she touched my hand, and how she told Karen the time. "Oh," I repeat, wondering at it all.

"Do you still want to go?" she asks.

This is a tough question. I mean ten seconds ago I was drooling at the possibility. Now, all of a sudden, my feet are freeze-dried. So is my brain. What is the matter with me? I mean, big deal, so she's blind. Which means she doesn't realize I'm really a fourteen-year-old geek whose panting she can probably hear. Which also really means all she wants to do is go for a boat ride. If I say yes, she'll think I'm being nice. If I say no, she'll think I'm prejudiced.

"Of course I want to go," I hear my nice self say. But as the words leave my lips, I realize I'm not so sure.

***

We're out on the middle of the lake, boogying along flat out in Dad's boat. Cynthia is grinning from ear to beautiful ear. Her dark hair is blowing in the wind. And she's *hanging on to my arm* as I drive. I'm feeling happy and sad at the same time.

On the beach, I can see that they've set up the commercial shoot. There's a camera and some guys holding big reflector things trying to catch the sun. There's also a crowd of girls. I wonder if Karen is among them. They're too far away to make out their faces. I decide to get closer. We can watch from the water — I can watch from the water — I'll describe it to Cynthia. This is my plan.

But Cynthia has other ideas.

"Have you got water skis?" she asks.

"What?" I mean I heard her, I just don't believe the question. I throttle the boat down.

"Water skis, you know, for skiing on the water."

"That's what I thought you said," I say. "Yeah. We have water skis."

"Do you mind if I go?"

"Water skiing?"

"Yes, water skiing. Would it be all right?" asks the Beautiful Blind Cynthia.

No. No, of course it wouldn't be all right! What's a blind person going to do water skiing? She'll fall down, fall in the water and drown, and I will be responsible. I'll be responsible for taking out the boat without permission from my dad and causing a blind person, a beautiful blind person, to drown in the lake. No, absolutely not. No water skiing.

"Please?" she asks, reading my mind. She tightens her grip on my arm.

"What happens if you fall in the water?" I ask.

"I can swim," says Cynthia. "I can probably swim better than you."

This is true. I'm lousy at it. But that's not the point.

"How will you know which direction to swim in?" I ask. "I mean, you might swim out into the middle of the lake, and then what?" I think I got her.

"I assume you'll make some sort of noise, Ken. I may be blind, but I'm not deaf."

I look into her sunglasses and see my reflection, a skinny, pointy-nosed geek with a bump on his head. "Sure," I say, "Why not." Line up the firing squad. Shoot me now.

Ten minutes later, we're ready to go. Cynthia's in the water, holding onto the tow rope, skis pointing skyward. I know what's going to happen. I'll ease the throttle up, and she'll collapse. This'll go on for three or four tries, then, that's it. She'll quit. And I'll be able to get the boat back, say good-bye, refill the gas tank and pray that Karen doesn't find out and tell Dad. I'm sure this is what's going to happen.

Not thinking about what I'm doing, I ease the throttle up at normal pace, like I've done a hundred times before. I look back and realize a terrible thing! I don't have a spotter, someone to check and make sure things are all right! And just as this thought is going through my mind, Cynthia rises out of the water and onto the skis, the first time! It took me ten tries to get up my first time. How can this blind person do it? She's incredible!

So now I'm trying to spot and drive the boat at the same time. Anybody who has ever done this knows that it is not only really dangerous, it is really stupid. But the truth is, Cynthia looks great. She's a natural and she is grinning like there's no tomorrow. Maybe there isn't. Because when I look towards where I'm heading with the boat, I see the beach full of wanna-be-stars, the camera guys, the two dudes with sunglasses, all looming up in front of me. *I've got to turn, fast!*

This I know is going to dump Cynthia in the worst possible place, i.e. in front of everybody on the beach. So be it. Life has to end sometime. I turn.

What happens next is this: Cynthia feels the direction change on the tow rope. She leans into the turn and cuts a spray six feet high, and whip cracks across the wake like a pro. I can't believe it. She doesn't go down. But it's enough for me. I head back to the dock a shaken man, well, *boy.*

"Wow, you're really good," I say as I'm putting stuff away.

"I know," she says. "I've been skiing since I was five."

"You didn't tell me that."

"You didn't ask. It's something I can do that's safe for me. I love it," says Cynthia, shaking her black hair. "Do I look okay?"

"You look fine," I say. She really does.

"My dad's meeting me at the Stones Throw. Would you walk me back?"

"Sure." The truth is I'll do anything for her, walk on hot coals, jump through fire, face the wrath of my dad . . . .

When we get there, Cynthia's father is waiting. He seems like a pretty good guy, for a father, and before I know it, she's in his car saying good-bye. I'm half-surprised that she's not driving.

"Will I see you again?" I ask, leaning into the car window.

"I hope so. I should be back in a week or two. You've been really sweet," she says and draws my head towards her and kisses me on the cheek. "Bye," she says. I bump my head taking it out of the car window and stand there dazed as the blue car drives off.

Blue. And a vague bit of black exhaust. Usually I can tell you the make, model and year. But not today. All I notice is that the car is blue, driving away with Cynthia.

***

I make it home and I'm calmly sweating, waiting to see if Dad's going to find out I took the boat today. He's out in the back, barbecuing steaks. Mom's getting a salad together. The only problem is Karen hasn't arrived.

"What happened to your head?" Mom asks.

"My knee gave out. I banged it."

"I told you to be careful," she says.

"Mom, it just goes whenever it feels like it. Being careful doesn't make any difference," I say. However, I *was* careful putting the boat away, and refilling the gas tank. So far, so good.

"Steaks will be ready in about five," says Dad, entering the cabin wiping his hands on his I'm-the-Cook apron. "So what did you do today?"

"Nothing. I met a girl."

"A *girl*," he says, his eyes opening wide.

"Well he's getting to that age," says Mom.

"What was her name?" asks Dad, always interested in the details.

"Cynthia," I say, realizing with a pang that I didn't even know her last name.

"Cynthia," says Mom. "That's an unusual name these days."

"She's really nice," I say. "Except she's blind."

"Blind?" they harmonize this, like a pair of backup singers.

"Yeah, you know, as in cannot see."

"That's . . ." Mom was probably going to say "interesting", but Karen slams through the door like a fullback, changing the direction of the ball game. "What happened to you?" asks Mom.

Karen plumps herself down on the big wicker chair, practically knocking the stuffing out of the cushion, adjusts her glasses and makes a sound like a whinnying horse. She knows how to get your attention. Karen's neat that way.

"I spend all day getting ready for this stupid audition, I go for the audition, I get chosen to be one of the girls on the beach. I rehearse this stupid scene where we have to run up and down the beach about a million times and I can't see anything because I'm not wearing my glasses, so I keep bumping into people and missing the place where we're supposed to stop."

Karen says all this in one breath. She gulps air and continues.

"So finally I'm embarrassed to death because the director takes me aside and explains things to me like I'm retarded, which maybe I am, because now we're doing takes with the camera rolling and I'm still screwing up."

Here she stops again, but this time it's more for emphasis.

"And finally after about fourteen takes, when I'm finally getting it right, some jerk comes roaring by in his boat with a water skier!" And she looks right at me.

"It wasn't me," I say.

"I know it wasn't you. You were with Cynthia," she says, then adds for Mom and Dad's sake, "She's blind."

"We heard," says Mom.

Yes! Yes! I was with Cynthia, and everybody knows that blind people can't ski. The perfect alibi! Thank you, Karen my beautiful sister. Thank you for not wearing your glasses. I want to kiss her, but I don't. That would be acting suspicious.

"Anyway," Karen continues. "The jerk goes by with the water skier, and the director and camera person and all the people who are in charge stop everything and have this huddle on the beach like this was a *football* game or something."

Karen hates football.

"Then they break up and tell us all thank you very much but we can go home." Karen is rolling her eyes in disbelief.

"That's it?" asks Dad.

"Yeah! That's it! Except we have to go back to the motel, get our stuff, then wait around for an hour and a half to sign these papers for some release or something. What a wasted day."

Wasted for Karen maybe, but I'm off the hook. I had a great day.

Everybody has sympathized with Karen and is now in the middle of trying to cut into Dad's burnt steak when a black van pulls into the yard. It's got Sunrise Films Inc. written on the side. Two people climb out. It's them, with the sunglasses and long hair. One of them still needs a shave. He has a video cassette in his hand. We're all wondering what's going on, especially me.

Dad answers the door.

"Is there a Kenny Martin living here?" asks Needs-a-Shave.

"Yes," says Dad. "He's right here."

Suddenly, I'm front and centre, chewing on a particularly tough piece of steak.

"We were shooting some footage for a commercial today and we just happened to get something that we're told you had a lot to do with." The steak is growing in my mouth. It is doubling in size and very dry.

"It's a shot of you on a boat and you're pulling a skier," says Doesn't-Need-a-Shave. I just about choke. Mom, Dad and Karen all stop, mid-chew. They look at me.

"We'd like to use it," says Needs-a-Shave, waving the cassette. "If we can get your permission."

"Can we see it?" asks Dad, all innocently. "I'm sure we'd all like to see it first."

"Surely," says Needs-a-Shave.

A few seconds later, there, on our TV, in livid colour, is me. There's no mistake about it. I'm wild-eyed, I crank the steering wheel. The camera pulls back, and there is Cynthia, shooting up a six foot spray. She is smiling.

It really is a great shot, but I'm dead meat.

***

To make a long story short, I make some money being in a commercial but can't really spend it because I've been grounded for a month. Grounding means no boat, a two kilometer fence and a nine o'clock curfew. It's really not that bad, no worse than last summer when I broke my knee, and especially now that I've got my guitar back. The only thing is, I can't turn up my amp.

So I spend a lot of time hanging out at the beach, when it's not raining, or at the Stones Throw with my buds, Snake and Jodie. Except they seem like such kids now. I mean they don't understand how I feel when I go there. All I can think of when I'm in the Stones Throw is Cynthia. It's like the place is haunted by her. Every time I walk in, I see her and it turns out to be someone else. Every time someone enters, I look up, hoping it's her. It's got to the point I don't want to go anymore, but don't dare not because it's the only place I'm likely to see her again. She said two weeks. About two weeks, and two weeks are up.

Mom and Dad are getting concerned. "How come you're not eating?" they ask. I don't know. I'm just not hungry. "Go do something with Jodie and Snake," they say. But Jodie and Snake are fed up with me, which is fine because I'm fed up with them too. I don't even feel like playing guitar.

I'm practically living at the Stones Throw now. I've started going alone and drinking coffee, with lots of milk and sugar. It lasts longer than coke and you can drink more because they give you refills, so you can spend more time there without getting kicked out. The waitresses look at me funny. It's two days over two weeks.

On the third day after two weeks, I'm at the beach skipping stones. It's a beautiful day. I hate beautiful days. The same two kids are on the beach building another sand castle. For some reason they're really noisy about it. They're having a ball. I want to tell them to shut up, that they've got no business having fun. They're just trying to bug me. I get half an urge to wring their scrawny necks. I see the headline, CRAZED YOUTH STRANGLES NOISY KIDS. I go up to the road instead.

A blue car passes, billowing black smoke. My heart leaps. Even though it's a cliché, my heart leaps when any blue car passes. My heart doesn't recognize clichés. It recognizes blue cars. This one pulls into the Stones Throw, a football field away. The black smoke settles. A man gets out. He crosses to the passenger side and opens the door. She gets out. It's Cynthia!

About twenty seconds later, I'm there. I would have been quicker but my knee gave out. My palms are scraped, my jeans are torn and I'm covered in dust. But I don't care. Cynthia's here.

She's sitting at a table with her father. She's beautiful. She's even more beautiful than I remember. It's a funny thing about memory. It doesn't work the way you expect it to. I push back my hair and approach. "Hi," I say.

"Hello?" she says with a question mark, looking up. I know she can't see me.

"It's Ken," I say. Maybe she can't remember who I am. Maybe she couldn't remember who I was even if she could see me.

"Oh hi, how are you," she says, holding out her hand. "Dad, you remember Ken. He took me water skiing. He's the one in the commercial."

"Yes, of course I remember. How are you, Ken?" He holds out his hand too. I take it. I'm standing there holding hands with two different people. I suppose I should shake them and let go. I do. "Would you care to join us?" asks Cynthia's father.

"Sure," I say. Is he kidding?

"In fact," he adds getting up, "why don't you join Cynthia while I go get the carburetor looked at? Let me know if you decide to do something."

"Okay Dad," says Cynthia.

He leaves and my mouth is full of swollen tongue. Or maybe it's heart. I swallow to try and get things back in place. But Cynthia speaks first.

"I've thought about you lots," she says.

"Me too," I say. "About you."

"That was fun we had, water skiing."

"Yeah, it was fun."

And here there's a pause where we try to figure out what to say next. I want to say I'm wildly and passionately in love with her, but I don't. Instead I finger-paint with some sugar that's spilled on the table.

"What are you doing?" she asks.

"I'm playing with some sugar."

She puts her hand on the table and sort of reaches across towards me. "Can I play too?"

"Sure," I pour sugar from the container, making a little cone on the back of her hand.

"It feels cool," she says.

I smooth the sugar out, spreading it evenly over the golden brown of her skin, part way up her wrist.

"That feels nice," she says.

I wet my finger with my tongue and touch the sugar, then put it back to my tongue. I do this fairly slowly, on different places, making little clear spots of skin surrounded by sugar.

"What are you doing now?"

"Making little islands of skin," I say. "Butterfly wings."

Cynthia smiles.

Shadow Dark Night

It's a big day around here. I've got a tingly feeling on my left side. Nurse Maureen is ecstatic. The doctors are impressed. This wasn't supposed to happen.

But then none of it was.

Nurse Maureen set an orange juice on the tray in front of me and then ran across the room to pick up Alex who just fell out of bed. Again. He does this all the time. If he doesn't watch it, they're going to strap him in. Anyway, the juice is about six inches from my mouth and I can't reach it.

I can't drink my orange juice — however, I can talk. What you're reading is a transcript of me talking into my tape recorder. It's voice-activated.

Actually, it's sound-activated. Any major sound sets it off. I leave it on all the time, even while I'm sleeping. When I wake up, I get Nurse Maureen to play it back for me. That way I don't miss anything. It's amazing what goes on here when I'm asleep. Last night Alex fell out of his bed twice.

The sound of Alex falling out of his bed is like a sack of potatoes hitting the floor. Not that I've ever heard a bag of potatoes hitting the floor, but I'm sure Alex is doing a good impression. Except for the little whimpering sounds he makes after. "Oh, oh, oh," he says.

Alex isn't too happy about being here. What exactly his problem is, I don't know, I mean aside from the fact that something is scrambled upstairs and he's lost the use of his legs. He's got two perfectly good arms.

Am I bitter, with nothing better to do than watching Alex fall out of bed? I was. There were days and nights I wished I was dead. If I could have figured out a way to kill myself, I would have. I tried not eating, but they flooded my useless arms with tubes of food. My parents let them. I hated them. I hated everyody. They wouldn't let me die.

Then Alex moved in. A body that works, with no mind to run it. And I think I've got it tough. I do. Except that he's got it tougher and doesn't even know it.

It's funny what gets you eating again.

The first day they set a food tray in front of Alex, he must have been hungry. He gobbled everything, using his hands. He's forgotten what forks and knives are for. That was lunch.

When they brought supper, he was far more creative in his gobbling. He flipped things up in the air and caught them with his mouth. It didn't matter what it was, potatoes with gravy, or little bitty peas, one at a time. Half of everything was on the bed and floor. It didn't matter. He chewed what he caught with this lovely look of peace on his face.

The next morning at breakfast, my birthday, he noticed me for the first time. He smiled. I guess he thought he should share his porridge with me. So he threw little handfuls across the room. Birthday presents. One of them actually hit me, on the nose. It trickled down to my mouth and I licked it in. It was good. I smiled at him with my brand new seventeen-year-old smile. He smiled back. That's what started me eating.

Nurse Maureen's been trying to teach Alex how to use a spoon and fork. He's got the idea that they have something to do with meals, but how they're supposed to help get food from the plate to his mouth is way beyond him yet. Usually he balances things on them. Or tries to. Like plates and cups. He's not very good at it.

I've been here six months now. My so-called friends stopped visiting long ago. The guys. Not that I particularly care. Most of the guys are a-holes anyway. They helped me get here. The only people who visit me now are my parents and my sister, Danielle. They help keep my spirits up. They take turns feeding me and watching the Alex show. Tonight Dad is feeding me.

Dad has always tried to do the right things for me. Right now it's easy, he can't make any mistakes, but when I was about eight or nine he packed me in the station wagon and took me out to the country. He was going to show me how to use a gun. I could hardly wait. This was big important business, the kind of stuff for men. My mom and sister stayed home in town and did whatever moms and sisters do when the men leave them to themselves. Probably knit and sew and stuff. Shop.

We drove to an abandoned gravel pit and there he unpacked me along with a brand new, single action twenty-gauge shotgun. We set up some cans and bottles along one wall of the pit and measured off forty paces from them. I had to jump from foot to foot to keep my paces the same length as my dad's. Then he lectured me about the safety catch, how you hold the gun and all those other boring things that you forget right away because all you want to do is pull the trigger and watch cans and bottles explode. Like in the movies.

Dad let me go first. He put the gun in my hands and told me to hold it tight against my shoulder because "the recoil might knock my arm off." I was amazed at how heavy it was, way heavier than my hockey stick which I'd been using as a pretend gun for as long as I could remember. Anyway, Dad told me to aim at one of the cans and squeeze the trigger real slow. Which I did.

What Dad never told me is how loud the bang is and how your head rings like somebody slapped you hard in the ear and how the recoil kicks the barrel skyward and slams the stock against your shoulder anyway, no matter how tight you hold the gun.

I didn't hit the can I was aiming at, but knocked three others over frontwards, the buckshot bouncing off the pit wall back towards me. This is what I guess happened because there is no other explanation for it. Anyway I stood there stunned and I turned to my dad. He smiled at me and took the gun from my hands. He said something to me, but I couldn't hear him because my ears were ringing, hurting, and all I did was run back to where the station wagon was parked.

I climbed inside and locked all the doors. I wanted the hurting and ringing to stop. I put my face onto the car seat and covered my ears with my hands. Dad had to practically break a window before I unlocked the driver's side to let him in.

We didn't talk on the way home, and when we got there, I found out that Mom and Danielle had been to a movie, *E. T.* Danielle couldn't stop talking about how good it was and what a great time they had. I tried to brag and tell her I knocked over three cans with one shot. I didn't tell her how. She told me how E.T.'s finger glowed when he made things feel better. She showed me, touching my finger with hers.

"Do you feel better?" Danielle asked.

How did she know I was hurting?

***

Alex is particularly talkative today. His eyes are wide and he's going a mile a minute. The only problem is, I can't understand a word he's saying. That's because he's not saying words. He opens his mouth and sounds come out. All gibberish. He seems to understand to a certain extent — he looks at you as if he does. Then he goes and balances a spoon on his nose. They're trying to do tests with him.

Nurse Maureen has given him one of those join-the-dots pictures that kids do — you know, with the numbers attached. She shows it to me now that he's done.

"What do you think, Dylan?" she asks.

What I see is an amazing series of scribbles.

"I think it's very nice," I say.

Alex is grinning from ear to ear. He's quite proud of his work. Maybe he sees dots that aren't there and joins them. It looks like something a two-year-old would do. Except Alex is in his mid-twenties, about the same age as Nurse Maureen.

Nurse Maureen tells me that there's nothing wrong with Alex's legs. He just forgot how to use them, like he forgot how to talk, use a fork and join dots with lines. The funny thing is that he can draw. Sort of. Everything he draws looks like it has been run over by a steam roller, very wide and flat. Alex looks okay, but that's because his hair's grown back. Underneath is a mass of scars where his head went through the windshield. That's what Nurse Maureen says.

I miss Maureen when she has days off. She has eyes that are always smiling, except when doctors are around. She hates doctors. So do I. That in itself is reason enough to like her. I especially like it when she is on nights. Sometimes when there's nothing to do but cry, she comes in here and strokes my face with the back of her hand. It's not sexy or anything like that, but it helps me not think of why I'm here.

This is what I cry about:

I'm lying face down on the floor. I see Kerrie's feet trying to step out of the blood. I can't feel anything. I hear Kerrie's slow screams from far away, yet I know those are his feet trying to step out of my blood.

***

It doesn't seem like anything much, but four of us are bored out of our skulls. Me, Kerrie, Jim and Duke. It's a hot afternoon and we're stuck in town while everyone else is at the lake. We're looking for something to do that doesn't cost anything because we're all broke and supposedly looking for jobs. All except Duke who has a job killing chickens for a meat-packing company.

Duke's twenty-one and always smells of chicken feathers. But he has money. And a car, a rust bucket. Today's his day off. He's sprung for a case of beer but hoards his smokes to himself. This bugs Jim to no end because Jim's the only other one who smokes. Kerrie and I could care less.

Kerrie and I go way back. We've been buddies since grade three. Kerrie's always been better than me at sports and girls, but I've had the edge in school and figuring out what to do next.

Anyway, Kerrie's uncle is a cop. We go to his place in Duke's car. We're at Kerrie's uncle's because he's on holidays and Kerrie is supposed to mow the lawn while he's away. Kerrie's uncle's is a good place to go on a hot summer day for two reasons: one, he's got a pool outside and two, he's got air-conditioning inside. It's also where we'd never go if Kerrie's uncle was home.

Kerrie's finished the lawn, and we've fooled around in the pool for a while, but now we're in the basement rec room drinking Duke's beer and listening to Kerrie's uncle's new CD player. He doesn't have much in the way of music, mostly country-and-western stuff that only Duke likes. Duke is happy. The rest of us are bored.

"He should have a pool table down here," says Jim.

"We could lift weights," I say, referring to one corner of the room where there's a little fortress of weightlifting gear.

"Too much like work," says Jim.

"You wanna play darts? There's a dart board," says Kerrie.

"No darts," says Jim.

"I wonder where he keeps them?" says Kerrie, and starts rummaging through drawers behind the bar counter.

"We could throw that axe," says Jim. Beside the fireplace is a small hatchet. "Pretend it's a dart."

"Forget it," says Kerrie.

"Why don't you guys shut up and listen to the music," says Duke.

"That's not music, that's puke, Duke," says Jim.

Everyone laughs.

"Hey! Look what I found," says Kerrie. And between his thumb and forefinger he holds a bullet.

He passes it around and we all hum and haw about what this could do to a guy, depending on where it entered your body and where it left, and depending on how far away it was shot from.

"So where's the gun?" asks Jim.

"What gun?" asks Kerrie.

"The gun that goes with the bullet, stupid," says Jim.

"I don't know," says Kerrie.

"I mean, your uncle's a cop, there must a gun around here somewhere. Let's find it," says Jim.

"What for?" says Kerrie.

"So we can see what it looks like!" says Jim, making it sound like it's the perfectly logical thing to do.

So we do it. We spread through the house like bugs, going through drawers and cabinets, looking in boxes and cases all over Kerrie's uncle's place.

"Don't mess anything!" yells Kerrie.

I'm in a room that's probably Kerrie's aunt's sewing room. It's full of that kind of stuff, like a bamboo box of thread spools, needles, measuring tape and scissors. In the middle is a large wooden desk like teachers have, with a

sewing machine on top. I open the bottom right hand drawer.
And there it is.

"I found it!"

Bare black. Lying on top of some pink flannel.

***

Quiet night. I think. I don't usually sleep all the way
through. Someone put one of Alex's drawings on my bed. I
can see upsidedown it's of Santa Claus. Filling the page.
Spread out like strawberry jam. It's actually pretty good in a
weird sort of way, except Santa's missing a mouth. I thank
Alex for it, but he's not paying attention.

Nurse Maureen puts it on my tray so I can see it better
then pushes the rewind button on my tape recorder so we can
find out what went on last night. The machine rewinds while
she gets me ready for my bath. She pulls the curtain around
the bed and gets me naked before the tape clicks to a halt. It
takes longer than usual to rewind.

"Ewww, what happened last night?" asks Maureen.

"I don't know, I slept."

"Maybe Alex fell out of bed."

"Yeah."

Maureen turns the machine on and starts washing me.
It's like she's washing somebody else, attached to my head. I
wish I could feel something. She's about to do my not-so-pri-
vate parts when we hear Alex's voice on tape.

Maureen and I look at each other. She stops washing me.
She covers me. We listen.

This is what Alex says.

"Slow. Oh. Ooh. Oooh. I like it when everything is slow. Shadow dark night when everything is slow. Not still, just slow. When everything is slow I can fool the moment that now is and stretch it long enough to start remembering. This is when I want to walk. I just about remember how. Slow. Ooh. Oooh. Ooooh."

Nurse Maureen yanks back the curtain. We look at Alex. Alex looks at us. He starts talking a mile a minute, without saying a word. He's waving his arms.

"Slow, Alex, slow," I say.

He tries to get out of bed and falls like a sack of potatoes.

***

We've got the gun in the rec room. Jim has put the bullet in one of the chambers of the revolver. You can see it. He points the gun at Kerrie.

"Hey, don't do that!" yells Kerrie.

Jim laughs, points the gun at the ceiling and pulls the trigger. The gun clicks.

"The bullet has to be in the right chamber," says Jim.

"We shouldn't be fooling around with that, you guys," says Kerrie.

"Who's fooling around?" says Jim. "We're examining it."

"It's dangerous," says Kerrie.

"It's only dangerous if you do this." And Jim puts the gun to his head. He pulls the trigger. Click. "Wow! What a rush."

"Jeez you're an idiot," says Kerrie. "That's Russian Roulette."

"No it's not. In Russian Roulette you go like this." Jim closes his eyes and spins the chamber. "Then you go like this." He points the gun at his head and once again pulls the trigger. Click. "YEAH!! HOLY SHIT, MAN!!"

"You didn't know where the bullet was?" I say.

"No way!" says Jim. "What a rush!"

"You're nuts, man — you're friggin' nuts," says Kerrie.

"Try it. I mean, don't knock it unless you try it," says Jim.

"Somebody's going to get hurt," says Kerrie.

"Here," says Jim. "You take it." He hands Kerrie the gun. "Now look where the bullet is, see? Nothing's going to happen to you, but I guarantee when you pull the trigger you get such a rush. It's like beating death. You beat the Reaper, man!"

"What do I want to beat the Reaper for?" asks Kerrie.

"The rush! The rush!" says Jim.

"Gimme," says Duke. He takes the gun from Kerrie, points it at his own head and slowly pulls the trigger.

Click.

"Oh YEAH!" he says. "It's a rush. Even when you know where the bullet is."

"Close your eyes and spin the chamber," says Jim.

Duke looks at the gun. Looks at everyone in the eye. Then closes his eyes and spins the chamber. His eyes still closed, he raises the gun barrel to his temple. As he squeezes the trigger, he slowly opens his eyes.

CLICK.

"AAAH!" he screams. "YEAH! YEAH!" he says, breathing hard.

"Come on, Dylan, you do it."

"I don't get along with guns," I say.

"Kerrie, you got to try it," says Duke.

"Come on, Kerrie," I say. "If you do it, I'll do it."

"All RIGHT!" says Jim.

Very reluctantly, Kerrie takes the gun. He checks the chamber, carefully. He points the gun to his head. He closes his eyes. He pulls the trigger. Slowly.

CLICK.

"GOD!" says Kerrie. "It really IS A RUSH. Even if you know."

Duke and Jim are laughing. It's the kind of laughing from nervous disbelief.

"Come on, Dylan, your turn," says Kerrie.

"Yeah," says Jim. "Don't be an a-hole."

"No, I can't do it," I say.

"Come on! You said if I did it, you'd do it."

"No. You do it for me."

"I'm not going to do it. You do it," says Kerrie.

"Just point the gun and pull the trigger."

"No."

I grab the gun by the barrel and stick it at the back of my neck. It is heavier than it looks. "Pull the trigger!" I yell.

I feel the weight coming off my hand. Someone has taken the gun. It is still at my neck. I drop my hand.

"Pull the trigger!" I yell. "Pull it! Do it now! COME ON, DO IT!"

The bang hits my ear like a baseball bat. I think of Dad.

I'm lying face down on the floor. I see Kerrie's feet trying to step out of the blood. I can't feel anything. I hear Kerrie's slow screams from far away, yet I know those are his feet trying to step out of my blood.

***

Alex left me another picture of Santa Claus. It's pretty much like the first one he did, broad, filling-the-page-too-wide. The only difference is that this Santa has a great big smile on his face. It's like the Cheshire Cat's smile in *Alice in Wonderland.*

Alex waves to me.

I wave back, slowly. With the little finger of my left hand.

The Rabbit

You have a dog named Rusty . . . you had a dog named Rusty. This is not so much a story about Rusty as it is about your parents, of which you still have two. That's because nobody's shot them, yet. You have this theory that parents are very stupid people, especially after you get to know them for awhile. You've known yours fourteen years. Fifteen, actually. The first year doesn't count.

If your dad was an animal, which you occasionally think he is, he'd be a bird. He'd be one that's nearly extinct, because it forgot how to fly. So he just flaps his wings and jumps instead, *jumps to conclusions.*

And your mom is like a pair of eyes that glow on the side of the road at night. You can't make out what they belong to, you just hope they don't spring across in front of the car. But one of these days, you know it's going to happen.

The thing is, you'd probably never notice how weird your parents are if you didn't have neighbours or other people to compare them to. For instance, the Unruhs, who live next door and have a rabbit.

It's a pet rabbit they keep in a cage beside the toolshed in the backyard. They feed it greens from the kitchen, and they recycle the little bunny turds, you know, throw them in the garden, where they grow their own organic food. They have a complete little eco-system over there — compost piles, solar heating panels, bird feeders — you name it. And just like the rabbit, the Unruhs are vegetarians.

You, on the other hand, have Rusty. Rusty is locked in his back yard prison. Every now and then, someone will leave the gate open and he will run madly all over the neighbourhood, sniffing and peeing on everything in sight. Doggy freedom. So leaving the gate open is a definite no-no in your house. Normally, however, he's stuck in the back yard where he dumps all over the place. When he's really bored, he eats it. Your job is to clean up before he does. Unfortunately, you're not very good at your job. Rusty has foul breath.

Rusty eats meat too, of course. He sits beside the barbecue, begging with his big sad piggy-doggy eyes, "Me too, me too," he's saying. He wants a piece of steak. If you break down and give him some, he sort of *inhales* it. He's more patient with sticks and shoes and plastic garden hose — those he chews on for a while.

You don't pretend to understand dogs. They're dogs. They do strange things. Rusty has dug up most of the lawn looking for bones, or China, or whatever dogs look for when they dig holes. Maybe he's just looking for a way out of the yard. It's like stepping through a minefield of holes and doggie-doo to get to the barbecue that pollutes the atmosphere with the smell of burning dead cows because you eat meat too. That's the kind of people you are.

Yet you are friends with the Unruhs, your rabbit neighbours. When you were little, you took swimming lessons together with their kids. Both sets of parents took turns chauffeuring you, your parents in your Ford, the Unruhs in their Volvo. They give you zucchini from their garden. Your mom makes five loaves of zucchini bread and you eat one. The rest she hides in the freezer.

One weekend the Unruhs go away. They have asked your Dad to keep an eye on their house. No problem. Three days. He can handle that.

It's evening of the second day, Saturday. You go to the video store to rent a movie. Nobody can agree on what movie to get so you get three. On the way home, you stop at the store for popcorn and coke. It's going to be fun, a family evening fighting over which movie to watch first.

But when you get home, driving into the driveway, black smoke belching from the Ford, you lurch to a halt and freeze. Your dad turns off the ignition. The exhaust settles like an air of doom. You know there is going to be trouble because *the gate is open.*

Rusty is gone.

You call, "Rusty, Rusty", you hope the dog remembers his name. He does. He appears, wagging his tail. He is wearing a foolish grin on his face.

Rusty has returned from the neighbour's yard. The Unruh's.

You go into their yard, and there, lying almost neatly on the compost pile, is a dead rabbit, a dirty dead pet bunny rabbit. You know now that Rusty is a killer. Your dad says if this is what Rusty will do to a rabbit, what might Rusty do to small children?

But Rusty is still standing there with that grin on his face, still wagging his tail. It's clear that Rusty is denying everything. He seems to be saying, "Is there a problem here?" Yes Rusty, there is a problem. Mentally, you can see your dad lining up the telescopic cross-hairs between Rusty's loving stupid eyes and shooting him. Except he can't.

This is where the story gets ugly.

Your dad puts Rusty in the car. Rusty thinks he's going for a car ride. He is. To the vet, who will do what your dad can't. You wave good-bye to Rusty. You thought he was such a good dog. Stupid, but good.

Meanwhile, your mom springs into action. Her eyes are like headlights, her face a grill. She takes the dead rabbit into the kitchen. She washes it in the sink, then takes her hair drier and blow dries the dead rabbit's fur. She fluffs it up. It looks almost as good as new. It really does.

By this time, your dad has returned from the vet. Your whole family is silent. Your dad takes the dead rabbit and puts it back into its cage. He props it up. He gives it a carrot. It looks like the dead rabbit is eating the carrot. You go home. You do not watch movies. You go to bed.

The next day the Unruhs return. Your dad gives them time to be home for awhile. Time to unpack the Volvo and put things away. There is no eye contact in your house. Your mom is trying to thaw a loaf of zucchini bread.

Your dad goes into the back yard and starts scooping up dog turds. You join him, holding a plastic garbage bag. Dr.

Unruh is in his back yard digging a hole. You hear your dad
ask, in a friendly neighbourly sort of way, how their trip was.
Dr. Unruh answers, it was fine, the trip was fine, but that
something really strange had happened here, here in the
back yard.

Your dad fakes great interest.

Dr. Unruh says that someone dug up their pet rabbit and
put it back into its cage.

Your dad's voice breaks. "Dug it up?"

"Yes," says Dr. Unruh, "It died last Thursday."

You look at your dad. He flaps his wings like he's trying
to fly.

"I didn't know," he says to you. "I didn't know."

Golfing With Mr. Death

I used to call my little brother "Bathtub Mouth" because he could never shut up. He would squeal on me every time I did something he thought Mom and Dad wouldn't like. He got me in trouble all the time, but I usually deserved it. His name was actually Cory.

He used to ask the most stupid, weird questions, like, "How come, 'how come' means *how come?*" Or, "Are the Blue Jays more Blue? Or are they more Jays?" Stuff like that. It would drive you nuts. But you had to admit, he had such a neat brain. I loved him.

I looked after him all the time because I was the brother closest to his age. I'm stuck in the middle. There's four years between me and the other two. My older brother, John, is in university, so I hardly see him.

What Cory and I did a lot was hunt for golf balls. I would wade out into the water hazards, just before dark and feel the balls with my toes. Then I would scoop them up with this invention of mine that consisted of one of Mom's ladles attached to a stick, and throw the balls to Cory on shore where he would put them in a bag. We'd take them home and wash them, then sell them to the golf pro as "Experienced Balls."

We made enough money that way to buy a partial set of clubs, with the three, five, seven and nine irons, plus a three wood and a putter. Cory would caddy for me and I would whack the ball around. We took it really seriously, like it was the Masters every time we went out. He liked caddying. He thought a caddy was part of a team, like the catcher in baseball, or the goalie in hockey. But really, he just got to carry all the clubs.

When you think about it, golf is a really stupid game. You whack a little white ball across a field and try to put it into a hole four inches wide. You try and do this eighteen times. That's how many holes there are on your average golf course. I suppose a perfect score would be eighteen, if you got a hole-in-one every time you hit it. But nobody has ever done this, eighteen times in a row. In fact, a pretty good score is four times that — seventy-two. It takes most people over a hundred whacks to do it. It takes me about seventy-five. It might be a stupid boring game, but I love it.

Cory was nine when he was diagnosed as having leukemia, and although nobody said anything about it, you could feel death creeping in around the house like some kind of fungus. You could almost smell it. I think the worst part was that nobody said anything about it. Death. They just pretended it wasn't there. Even when John, my older brother, did a bone marrow transplant.

This is something you do when somebody has cancer of the blood, which is what leukemia is. You get somebody who has the exact same blood type, which wasn't me — it was John — and you scrape out the marrow and put it in the dying person. You do this because bone marrow is where blood is made. Sometimes it works. And sometimes it doesn't.

It didn't work for Cory. And it didn't affect the fungus feeling. In fact, it somehow made it worse.

I think it spread.

From Old Man Farley's.

***

Although I see him mostly at the golf course, Old Man Farley is a neighbour of ours. He's always working in his yard, or if he sees you doing something, he'll wander over and offer to help, or worse, advise you. I mean he can't help much because he's not in very good shape, in fact he looks like he's going to croak any minute. The truth is, he's looked that way for as long as I can remember.

The weird thing about him is that he's always laughing and joking around. You wonder why — I mean his wife died last year, and the year before that, his daughter. They both got hit by the big C. Talk about fungus. I can't believe how he stays so cheerful because if my family was dying all around me I doubt if I'd find life a pile of yucks. But there he is.

The other thing he does is golf, which is the only thing he complains about, how he has never shot a hole-in-one. When he's not poking around the weeds in his yard or giving some neighbour advice on just how deep that post hole should be, he's out puttering around the golf course. So am I.

Ever since my dad took me and Cory golfing when I was ten, I've been a hopeless addict. I should be locked up in a padded room. There should be a line-up to throw the key away. My dad would be the first in line. He's sorry he ever took me. I beat him all the time now. I also beat my older brother and just about anybody else who's a member at Bluebryre Golf and Country Club.

The only person I can't beat is Old Man Farley.

Now you've got to get the picture here. Old Man Farley is not a good golfer, he's not even average. In fact, he's a terrible golfer. And there's a good reason for this — he doesn't have any hips. Well, he *has* hips, but they're artificial and every couple of years, he goes in for replacements. He's gone through three or four sets now, and he's only seventy. He gets around with canes and a golf cart. *Everybody* beats him, all the time. Everybody, that is, but me. I can't figure it out.

***

My dad says I spend too much time at the golf course. He's right, I do. I'm there all the time. When I'm not washing clubs or gathering range balls, or filling the ball washers and water coolers, I'm in the practice bunker hitting sand shots, or maybe trying to hit a long iron clean from a tight lie on the range. This is when I'm supposed to be home, doing other stuff, like mowing the lawn and painting the fence.

So I'm not surprised he gets a bit upset when I tell them I'm entering my fifth tournament of the summer.

"When are you going to do something around *here?*" asks Dad.

"Like what?" I ask back. Two can play this game.

"Like *anything*," says Mom.

"I do stuff," I say.

Dad gives me that who-are-you-kidding look.

"I stay out of your way," I say. This is my attempt at humour. It doesn't go over real big.

"You think that's funny, do you?" Dad says, "Well I'll tell you what's funny. You're funny well grounded until you can funny well figure out something to do around here!"

It suddenly seems real tense, like Cory Bathtub Mouth has just squealed on me for something. But it's just me being caught for being lazy. The only way to break the tension is to have some sort of agreement. It's either that or stay grounded.

So we make a deal. I agree to mow the lawn and paint the fence — they agree to let me play in the tournament.

Except it's not that simple. We have an eight-foot fence that surrounds three sides of our yard and I have only one day to do it before the tournament, plus mow the lawn.

This is a fairly huge job and I don't even know if it's possible, but it's the best deal I can strike. I think about wimping and whining, but I know I'm not going to get any sympathy. If Cory was around, I could probably con him into helping. But he isn't. My older brother has a regular job, so I can't look to him. He would tell me to get lost anyway.

I pretty well accept my doom when out of the blue I get help.

From Old Man Farley.

***

The first time I played old Farley was a couple of years ago. I wasn't as good then as I am now, but I was certainly good enough to beat an old guy with two canes.

It was a beautiful day, the birds were singing, the sun was shining and a gentle breeze was keeping the bugs down. Off in the distance you could hear the mowers cutting the seventeenth green.

Farley was wearing black pants with a sweater to match. It was kind of hot for black and not what he usually wore — red plaid. I made some stupid crack about how he was dressed for a funeral, and he said, "Yes, I am actually — my daughter's."

I looked him in the eye. He wasn't kidding.

"She died three years ago today," he said.

Cory had been buried six months before.

He teed it up, sort of propped himself up on his two canes and whacked the ball about twenty yards. I boomed my drive two-sixty down the middle. "Great shot," he said.

It took him about three more whacks to get to where my ball was, and all the while he was talking about what a great funeral his daughter had, and how she weighed seventy-three pounds when she died, and how she hated the wig she had to wear after the chemotherapy left her with no hair. He wasn't doing this in a depressing kind of way, he was talking about it as a matter of fact, like a visit from a friend.

I lined up my second shot and pulled it just left of the green. "Great shot," he said, "just a little left. I always pull them left now that my right hip's gone."

I scuffed my chip two feet, leaving it worse than it was. He landed within twenty yards of the green and holed his chip shot. I eventually got it down for a six — we tied the first hole.

On the next hole I was so determined not to go left that I shanked my ball right, out-of-bounds. "Great swing," said Farley, "just a little right. I used to do that a lot too, till they replaced my left hip."

He went on to mention how they took three tries to get his *left* hip *right* and chuckled at his own bad pun. Then he started banging himself around the waist with one of his crutches. "I think one of these dang pins is working loose," he said. I half expected one of his legs to fall off.

By the time we came up the eighteenth fairway, it was taking me two or three hacks to move the ball thirty feet. I was mush. It was like I was swinging a two-by-four trying to hit a pea.

"Great game," said Old Man Farley when we were done, "I think I got you." I had stopped keeping score after the twelfth hole. I can't add that high.

It was a year later the next time I played him. I was a year older, a year wiser, and a year better. But his wife had just died. I heard all about it, how she weighed only seventy pounds, how her hair all fell out, how she started to look like wax. Cheerfully, matter-of-factly, he did it to me again. It wasn't quite as bad as it was the year before, but it was bad enough. Farley shot a hundred and three, and beat me by five strokes.

I started thinking of him as Mr. Death.

***

It's the day before the tournament and I've been up since six A.M. knowing it's going to be a real race for me to get the fence done. You can hardly tell I started and it's already ten o'clock. I wish I had a spray gun to speed things up. Or help. Help would be good too. And like an answer to my prayers, Old Man Farley hobbles up.

"Need a hand?" he says.

"Yes," I say. Even though Mr. Death isn't ideal as far as help is concerned, he's better than nothing. "I've got to do the whole fence." I'm probably whining, but I don't care.

"What you need is my spray gun. I'll go get it."

"Great!" I say. I try not to jump up and down.

For a guy who's all shackled by a couple of canes, Old Farley gets around pretty good, mostly on his golf cart. In a couple of minutes he shows up with the sprayer, a bunch of hose and a compressor all loaded into the cart. He's grinning from ear to ear. The question I ask myself is, why is this guy so happy?

"So," he says, "I see you're in the tournament tomorrow."

"Only if I get this done. And mow the lawn." I'm hauling hose out of the cart.

"With this gear we'll be done before lunch. Here, grab this," he says.

I pick up one end of the compressor and we set it on the ground. Just then Kaitlin Anthony walks by on the other side of the street. She's a neighbour about my age. We go to school together. She waves.

"That your girl friend?"

"No, we're just friend friends. I don't have a girl friend."

"A good looking guy like you? When I was your age I had three or four," he says chuckling. "'Course I had a lot more time than you — painting fences, golfing, you're a busy guy."

"Yeah, I don't have much time."

"You get to be my age you'll have lots more time. The only problem is the girls aren't too interested in you any more. You start shrinking." He chuckles again.

I smile my plastic smile. I'm not sure where this is heading.

"You start shrinking, then you disappear altogether. Some morning I'm going to get up and I'm not going to be there," he says, laughing outright. "Soon too," he adds.

I'm not sure what's so funny, but all of a sudden he stops and asks, "You see the pairings for tomorrow?"

"No." It immediately occurs to me that I don't want to know.

"Well, it looks like you and me, kid, if I'm still alive."

This complete feeling of dread comes over me. It feels like someone has filled my veins with ice water, or embalming fluid. Somebody has. It's Old Man Farley. Don't get me wrong, I like the old guy, or admire him in a bizarre sort of way. I just hate what he does to my golf game. I'm determined not to let anything he says bother me, I don't care who's died. I should be in luck because he doesn't have any more relatives. But I'm wrong. There's him.

For the next two days, or hours, or whatever time it takes for us to spray paint the fence, old Farley tells me about how he is dying. About how his plastic hips are causing some kind of cancerous growth and how this growth has spread to his lungs. He tells me that this is the last fence he will ever paint.

He tells me this is the last summer he will ever play golf. This he is not cheerful about. This makes him sad.

And tomorrow I play him, Mr. Death.

I don't eat much supper and I go to bed really early. Mom comes down to my room and asks what's the matter. I tell her I'm just tired. I can tell she doesn't believe me, but what can I say? There's some stuff you've just got to work out by yourself. But I don't know how. I know I'm going to lose even before I start, and even if by some miracle I can play my regular game, how can I beat a guy who's dying?

I cry instead, thinking of Cory, the last time he caddied for me. He wasn't a very good caddy, he used to have to practically drag the clubs around the course, but he was really into it. He knew the distances, the best places to land your ball, like *the little dip* in front of the seventeenth hole. And I'm back out on the golf course, the last time we went out, Dad and me and Cory with the hair chemoed off his head covered with a Blue Jay hat and his big brown eyes knowing what's going to happen, that he is going to die. He knows this. Yet he still smiles and says, "Hit that dip, Jason! Hit it right there and it'll go in." And in my half-dream I do hit it there, but I never see the ball go in the hole because I fall asleep.

About three in the morning I wake up like I was hit by a bolt. I know exactly what I'm going to do tomorrow. I'm going to lose to Old Man Farley — on purpose.

***

It's just about a quarter to eight the next morning and I've been on the practice tee warming up since seven-thirty.

I'm not warming up like most people, I'm *trying* to make bad shots. But I'm nervous and feel lousy because I didn't sleep too well. Out of the corner of my eye I watch for Farley. I don't want him to see me *practising*. I begin to worry that we'll miss our starting time. But just as they announce our names on deck, out he wheels from behind the clubhouse and pulls up to the first tee. He's wearing his red plaid pants. For an old guy dying of cancer, he looks great.

"Beautiful day!" he says. And it is, it's perfect. Except for a grey rim of cloud on the horizon.

I mutter something in agreement and ask if he'd like to tee off first.

"Beauty before age, kid! You show me the way."

I tee it up, get set, and nail the ball two-sixty down the centre. I didn't mean to, it just happened, honest.

"Oh, is that how it's done" says Mr. Death. "Well poop, I can do that." He doesn't, of course, but gets it about a hundred yards out. One of his better shots.

I set up for my second shot, planning to scuff it thirty feet, but I miss. The ball lands two feet from the cup. I tap in for a birdie.

Then he starts. He tells me that when he was two, his parents died. He moved in with an aunt and uncle. They died two years after that. And on and on. Anyone he was ever close to, died. Some died slowly, some fast. Till now, it is his turn. He is cheerful because it will all be over soon.

As he is telling me this, the clouds start rolling in, and by the fourteenth hole you can hear thunder in the distance. But through it all, *I can do nothing wrong*. The harder I try to screw up, the better the shot is. I've shot thirty-three on the front nine. It's unreal. If I keep going at this pace, I'll shoot my best round ever.

Rain is falling as he says, "Great game, kid. You have one of the most beautiful swings in the world." I want to hug him, but I don't. I'm such a coward. And besides I'd get even wetter.

We're now on the seventeenth hole, which is a little par three. It's simple enough, with bunkers to the left, a big poplar tree to the right and a green that slopes away from you. But the thunder is close and lightening flashes are all around. The siren has sounded from the clubhouse warning all golfers to come in. Old man Farley says, "Just two more holes. Let's finish up."

In front of the green, just off the fringe, is that little dip that if you catch just right, will cause your ball to roll to the right rear of the green, where the pin is usually placed, where it is today. It's a good spot to aim for.

I take out an eight iron, and just as I'm about to hit the ball, a crack of thunder splits the air, and I pull the shot left of the green to the bunker.

"Bad break, kid," Old Farley says and lines up his canes, trying not to slip on the wet grass. He knocks a five iron pretty good. It's high enough and hits the little dip in front of the fringe. The ball bounces right and rolls across the green, nudges the flagstick and falls into the hole!

A hole-in-one!

I don't know if you've ever seen an old man jumping up and down with two canes and a five iron before, but it's quite a sight. Old Man Farley's about the happiest guy on the planet.

It takes him a minute or two to get settled, to get his ball out of the cup and kiss it. But soon enough he's waiting for my bunker shot, holding the flagstick for me. "Knock 'er in!," he says to me with a big happy grin on his face, when crack! Like God's hand, a flash of lightening explodes out of the sky and hits the tree forty feet away. Old Man Farley tumbles like a bowling pin.

I race to him lying there in the rain. He turns to me, blinks a couple times and says, "Must have roots that come under the green. Better finish up, kid, before the next one gets us."

"No!" I say, "I've got to get you to the clubhouse!"

"Finish up!" He says, "You quit now and you'll forfeit the game!"

"No!" I repeat, "You need to get to the clubhouse!"

"You want me to beat you again? Finish up, I'll be all right."

So, I do. I chip in for a birdie. I batter my way through the rain on eighteen with Old Man Farley nodding and smiling on the golf cart beside me. I finish with my best round ever, a sixty-seven.

As we wheel towards the clubhouse he leans against me, and with rain running down his face, he says, "Bury me there." I don't know what he's talking about.

He looks back across the golf course through the rain towards seventeen where he shot his hole-in-one and says, "Take my ashes and bury them there, in *the little dip.*"

***

Half the Bluebryre Club came to his funeral and the seventeenth hole is more difficult to par now that the little dip is gone.

It's been a year since Old Man Farley died. Sometimes when I'm out here really early in the morning, just as the mist is lifting, I swear I see him off in the distance of the seventeenth hole. He doesn't have his canes. He has the most beautiful swing in the world. And guess who his caddy is?

Toy Boat

Now that the snow is going my little sister and her friends find a dry patch of sidewalk and drag out their skipping ropes. Us guys are caught between playing hockey, because the play-offs haven't quite started yet, and looking for our ball gloves somewhere in the basement. Spring is coming soon.

So is Aunt Ellen. She always shows up around Easter. For some reason it seems like a bigger deal this year. Especially for Zinny.

Until Dad gets home from work, my job is to look after Zinny. She's nine, I'm fourteen. There are some times you got to admire little kids. They get their single-track minds going, and you can't stop them till they get what they want.

Anyway, I'm sitting outside trying to catch some of those early spring rays and Zinny's skipping with some friends. I don't normally watch nine-year-olds skip, but it's the only place where there's sun and to tell you the truth I'm kind of impressed. They're in pretty good shape, I mean, for girls, and they all know these skipping songs. Imagine trying to play hockey and sing at the same time.

It's Zin's turn at turn at skipping. She sings her favourite song.

> *Three, six, nine,*
> *The goose drank wine*
> *The monkey chewed tobacco*
> *On the street car line,*
> *The line broke*
> *The monkey got choked*
> *And they all went to heaven*
> *In a little toy boat.*
> *Tell it loud and tell it bold,*
> *How many people did it hold?*
> *(Pepper) Ten, twenty, thirty . . .*

It's as far as she gets before she trips on the rope.

"Aw nuts," she says and goes to her friend Kim and takes the end of the rope from her. "Your turn."

Kim is one of those kids who thinks she knows everything and who already wears nylons and whose older sister is a cheerleader and whose mother sells Avon door-to-door, so you know she's very into *how things look.* She rolls her eyes and says to Zin, "That song is so dumb."

I have this instant urge to get up and strangle her because I kind of like the song myself, but all Zinny says is "Oh yeah? *Why?*" like she's really actually curious.

"Because," says Kim, "You don't go to heaven in a toy boat. You grow wings when you die and you fly there."

This is news to me, not that I believe you go to heaven in a boat, but you don't grow wings and fly there either.

"Who said?" asks my sister.

"My mom," says Kim.

"My mom's dead," says Zin. She says this so matter-of-fact, that it shuts Kim up. It happens to be true and Kim knows it. There is no more to be said.

It's after supper and Dad has turned the kitchen into a workshop. I'm helping him put together one of those book-shelf kits. Dad is not a carpenter. Neither am I. Dad is trying to read the instructions while holding all the pieces together. I'm trying to find all the screws.

The bookshelf will be for Zin. Because she loves reading, she has a zillion books and nowhere to put them. She is in the stairwell doing something — out of sight, but we can hear her. You can always *hear* Zinny.

"Dad?"

"Not now, Zin, I'm busy."

"I just want to ask you a question."

"What?" Dad is losing his patience.

"When's Aunty Ellen coming?"

"For the tenth time . . . tomorrow!"

"No, I mean, what time?"

"Zinny!!" He yells. Then he turns to me, "Haven't you found all the screws yet?"

"Were there supposed to be seven big ones, or eight?"

"Eight!" He doesn't yell this, but he might as well.

"There's only seven," I say. It's all I can find.

"Dad?" It's Zinny again. She's going to get us both killed.

"Hey, do you want a bookshelf or don't you?"

Suddenly there is a loud clunking. Zinny rolls into the kitchen clutching at the walls. She is wearing her new in-line roller blades.

"I can't get the laces tight."

"Zinny you're nine-years-old, you can tighten . . . Watch out!"

Zinny loses her balance and grabs at the nearest thing, which happens to be the bookshelf. The whole thing crashes down. On top of me. It is suddenly very, very quiet. You can hear one of the rollers on Zinny's skate turning.

"Oops," she says. "I fell."

"No kidding," I say, picking boards off myself.

"Now you know why I didn't want you in here," says Dad.

"I'm sorry," says Zin and she starts crawling away. Dad picks her up and puts her on a chair.

"How many times do I have to tell you, no roller blades in the house?"

"I was only . . . " She doesn't get a chance to finish.

"Do you want me to put them away? Is that what you want?"

"No," she says with a little tiny pathetic voice. She's good at that.

"Well then take your roller blades outside. You've got all outdoors to crash around in!"

"I just wanted to practise for when Aunty Ellen gets here!"

"Outside!"

"It's freezing winter outside!"

"It's not freezing winter, it's the middle of April — stop exaggerating all the time."

"Then, why is it snowing out?"

Dad crosses to the window and looks. She's right. It is snowing. It was sunny this afternoon, but now it's snowing. Dad continues to look out the window. I know what he is thinking. He is thinking about Mom.

Zinny crosses to him, wobbling. She clutches on to him.

"Dad?"

"Huh?"

"When Aunt Ellen comes, can we paint Easter eggs?"

"Mm-hm."

Zin and Dad both stand there, staring out the window. I want to join them, but there are times when you've got to leave your little sister and your dad alone, together.

"Was it snowing like this when Mom died?" asks Zin.

"Just like this," says Dad.

"How did she get to heaven?"

"Huh?" Dad asks.

"I mean, did she grow wings and fly up?" These are typical Zin questions.

Dad shrugs his shoulders, "I don't know — why?"

"Kim's mom said that's how you go."

"She did, huh? Well if you're going, I guess you might as well fly."

"That's what I'm going to do. And see Mom. How come you have to die first?"

This makes Dad pause. It's such a stupid question, on the surface. But if you mull it over for awhile, it really makes you think.

"I don't know, Sweetheart — those are the rules, that's all . . . Pretty stupid rules, huh?"

Zin nods in agreement. "Yeah. I wish she was here."

"Me too," says Dad.

I don't say anything.

***

It's a major chore trying to get Zin to go to bed, especially when I'm babysitting her, like I am tonight. She is such a slob. She leaves a trail of things lying all over the place. I found this letter in the bathroom.

> *Dear Zinny,*
> *I'm glad to hear that you're pleased with your roller skates. Perhaps if I can find a pair to fit, we can go out together and terrorize the neighbourhood. Looking forward to seeing you and Jodie and your Dad on Easter.*
>
> *Your loving Great Aunt, Ellen.*
>
> *P.S. By the way, here is a dandy two-word tongue twister for you — Zeus's Zithers*

I try to say it a couple times myself. "Zeus's Zithers." It is a good one. Zinny will walk around practising these things for — well, I was going to say days, but she doesn't do anything for that long, it just seems that way, it's really — minutes. She's quite good at it. She and Aunt Ellen have this tongue twister contest they've played ever since I can remember. It a carry-over from when Mom and I would play tongue twister when I was little. I'm pretty good at it too.

But right now, I have to get her to bed. Tomorrow Aunt Ellen arrives.

"Zin! What did Dad say about leaving all these books lying around?" Her room looks like it's been dumped upsidedown. It's worse than mine. And *she's* got a bookcase.

"I can't decide what order to put them in," she says. She's kneeling on the floor in front of it.

"Yeah, well do it tomorrow. Did you brush your teeth?"

"I've got to do this *now*," she says.

I know there is no point in arguing with her because she always wins anyway, so I get down on my knees and start shoving books onto the shelves.

"Not there," she says, grabbing an old *Dr. Seuss* book from me. "Here."

I know this is going to be a long night, so I just pass books to her and let her put them where she thinks they belong. I try to make conversation.

"You left your letter in the bathroom."

"What letter?"

"Zeus's Zithers."

"Oh, from Aunt Ellen. Yeah, I guess I forgot it there. I was practising."

"In the bathroom?"

"What's wrong with that?"

"Oh nothing. Most of us do *other stuff* in the bathroom."

"I was doing *other stuff* at the same time."

"Yeah, okay." She can get really huffy. "So, can you say it?"

"Say what?"

"What you were *practising*!"

"No. Not fast, anyway. I can't think of any good ones for her either."

"I've got one."

"Yeah?"

"Toy boat."

"Toy boat, that's easy."

"Say it fast."

"Toy boat, toyboyt, toeboot ... BAA!"

"Told ya."

"It *is* a good one. 'Toy boat, toy boyt', I can't even get past two! Thanks, Jodie. I'll get her with that one."

In a few minutes we have put the books onto the shelves and Zinny has finally said her prayers and climbed into bed. I'm just about to turn out the light in her room when she says, "Jodie, what's a hickey?"

I just about fall over. "What's a *what?*"

"A hickey?"

"I don't know. Ask Dad." I *do* know. I just don't want to talk about hickeys with my nine-year-old sister.

"I did ask him. He won't tell me."

"Well, if he won't tell you, why should I?"

"Because you're my brother."

I hate it when she does stuff like that. What difference does it make that I'm her brother? It's no excuse to talk about hickeys.

"Go to sleep," I say.

"I mean, I know it's a red mark, but how do you get them?"

"Yeah, it's a red mark. Good night."

"Have you ever had one?"

"Yeah. No. Never mind! Zin, what do you want to know this for?"

"Kim's sister has one." Figures.

"Listen, it's a mark you get . . . when you, ah, suck your skin . . . too hard."

"On your *neck?*"

I can't believe this. "Yeah, sometimes, yeah."

"You *did* have one didn't you?"

"Zin, good night!"

I get out of there before I do any more damage to my reputation about which I have never thought before. It's as though my reputation could ruin her reputation, especially since she's way too young to have one. You've got to be careful what you say to little kids.

She always asks the weirdest questions. Like she wanted to know if she was born when Mom died. It doesn't take much thinking to figure that one out. I laughed when she asked it, but I shouldn't have. She really meant it. And she really meant it when she asked what it feels like when you die. How do you talk about stuff like that with little kids? Or even big kids? I mean, what are you supposed to say? Dad says it's not a good thing to talk about. "Not now, Sweetheart," he says. "When you're older, you'll know." How much older?

Aunt Ellen was Mom's Aunt, which technically makes her my great aunt. And she really is a *great* aunt. She's probably in her seventies but you'd never guess by the way she looks and acts. She has this slogan — "You're only as old as you feel and I don't feel any older than you," she says, no matter who she is talking to.

When she arrives and we pick her up at the airport, we're hardly in the car when she and Zinny are doing their tongue-twister routine. "Zeus's Ziscors, Zeus's Thizers," and "Toy Boat, Toy Boyt, Toe Boyt" Etc. They laugh like a couple of kids. One of them is a kid. The other just thinks she is.

After supper, Dad goes to the store to get egg decorating stuff and leaves the three of us doing dishes. Zin likes soap bubbles, foaming like Niagra Falls. You can hardly find the sink, let alone the dishes. Normally she manages to shoot about five spurts from the soap bottle while no one is watching. But I catch her, mid-squirt.

"Zin, don't use so much soap!" I say.

"It just comes out like that," she screams at me.

Aunt Ellen looks at me and with a half-turn of her head pointing to the living room, indicates to me that I should go. I do. I sit in the big chair and turn on the TV, but keep the volume low so I can hear what they're saying.

"It just comes out, and then he gets mad," says Zin.

"Yes, well, men can get pernickity sometimes."

There is a pause here, and all you can hear are dishes clinking. Then Zin says something that makes me want to jump out of the chair and do dangerous things. But I hold back. This might be interesting.

"Do you know what a hickey is?" she says.

"A what? A *hickey*? No, what is it?"

"It's a mark you get from sucking your arm . . . or your neck."

"Oh, I didn't know that. How interesting . . . Who told you that?"

"Jodie . . . He knows lots of stuff like that."

"Yes, I bet he does, doesn't he?" Aunt Ellen says this a little louder than she needs to. Just to make sure I hear.

"I think Dad knows too, but he won't tell me. He won't tell me anything."

"Oh, like what?"

"Like what happens when you die. I asked Dad, and he says wait till you get older."

"Well I'm not sure anybody knows."

"Kim's mom says you grow wings and fly."

"Really."

"Is that true?"

"I don't think so, but I really don't know."

"And you don't go in toy boats either, right?"

"Well who knows, maybe you do. But I know one way you can't go."

"How?" asks Zinny.

And here Aunt Ellen starts singing,

> *Oh you can't get to heaven, oh you can't get to heaven,*
> *On roller skates, on roller skates,*
> *Or you'll roll right by, or you'll roll right by,*
> *Those pearly gates . . .*

"Oh! Can we go roller-blading tomorrow?"

"Tomorrow? Well, we'll see, okay?"

"You said in your letter we'd go."

"I didn't say no, Sweetheart. I just said we'll see. Your old aunt might want to take it easy for a couple days."

"Yeah, but when Dad says *we'll see*, it means *no*."

Aunt Ellen starts laughing here and says, "Okay, yes, we'll go. Definitely."

"All right! Jodie? Did you hear that? Aunt Ellen and I are going roller-blading tomorrow."

All of a sudden, I hear a crash. I jump up and run to the kitchen. There, lying on the floor, is a shattered plate!

"Oh dear!" says Aunt Ellen.

"That's okay, I'll get a broom." I cross to the broom closet.

"Be careful, don't step on any glash," she says, like her false teeth have come loose. "Old butter fingers here."

"It's okay Aunty, I do it all the time," says Zin. And she's right. She does.

Aunt Ellen sits down on a chair. She is biting her lower lip. Her face is white. That's when I remember that my Dear Old Aunt has all her own teeth.

***

Aunt Ellen is staying in the "guest room". It's right next to mine. Dad keeps yelling at me to turn my CD player down when I hardly have it turned up at all. Now I know why. The walls are paper thin. You can hear conversations in the next room. It's one thing to eavesdrop on what people say deliberately. It's something else to do it accidentally. There are some things you just don't want to know.

It's about ten-thirty and I'm lying in bed reading a book that's too thick and too heavy and I can't get into it. But somebody gave it to me and I promised that I'd read it. All of sudden I hear a knock. I think it's at my door, but it isn't. It's at Aunt Ellen's. I hear her ask Dad to come in. I rest the book on my chest.

Zin has made Aunt Ellen an Easter Egg. I saw it this afternoon. It's quite a feat, covered in rainbows and balloons with a toy boat painted on it. It's supposed to be a secret, so I don't know why Dad is showing it to her now. They talk about it for a while, then how I'm such a "good big brother to her" and other complimentary stuff that kind of makes me blush, even to myself. If they knew the times I felt like strangling her. But then the conversation changes.

"She looks so much like her mother," says Aunt Ellen.

"Yes . . . I look at that little face sometimes and all I can see is Karen . . . and Zinny's been going through a funny thing lately. I don't know if I should be concerned or what."

"Oh?"

"Yes, she keeps talking about death and dying — that sort of thing. I mean, it's morbid coming from a nine-year-old."

"She'll be ten soon."

"A ten-year-old, then — it's still morbid."

"Have you talked to her?"

"Well . . . what can you say? I mean, with Jodie it was different. He was there. He was old enough to know what was going on. But life is tough enough. Kids shouldn't have to face that . . . they should teach it in school or something."

"We all have to learn about it sometime, Stevie — maybe *they* should teach it at home."

"What am I going to do?" Dad's voice goes higher. "Take her to the morgue? Drag out the forensic pictures of Karen *after* she went through the windshield? With her broken neck? Her face that looked like, like . . ."

And now there is no more talking. Just muffled sounds.

I can hear Aunt Ellen saying, "It's okay, Steve. It's okay."

I know my Dad is crying. This is when I start crying too.

***

It's Easter Sunday. We spent the morning eating chocolate and searching through the basement for Mom's old roller skates. I found my ball glove. Zin found the skates. They have metal wheels and weigh a ton. But now Zin and Aunt Ellen are outside rolling up and down the sidewalk, Zin on her new roller blades, Aunt Ellen on Mom's old roller skates.

I am sitting in the big chair, channel surfing, trying to find something worth watching, while eating half a chocolate bunny, the top half. Dad is standing at the window, eating the bottom. Either he doesn't mind or he hasn't noticed. You'd never guess he had a care in the world. He's just standing there eating a chocolate bunny bum and smiling.

All of a sudden, his face snaps wide open. A look of shock. He drops the chocolate and runs to the door. I jump up and look out the window.

Aunt Ellen is crumpled on the sidewalk. Zinny is on her knees beside her, screaming.

***

After the ambulance came, we went to the hospital and waited and waited for some kind of word, but no one would tell us anything. Every few minutes Dad would get up and go to the counter where the nurses were, then he'd come back with this hopeless look on his face. Till finally, the nurse said we should go get something to eat. We'd been there all afternoon and it was after six.

I knew I was hungry but I didn't feel much like eating. Neither did Zinny or Dad. We poked around our plates at cold chips covered in gravy that looked like it was forming a plastic skin.

"Eat up," said Dad. "I'll take you home, then I'll come back and wait myself."

"No," said Zin.

"Zinny, it's been a long day." He wanted to continue but Zin started crying.

"What's the matter, Sweetheart? Huh?"

"Nothing . . . I hate roller blades."

"You hate roller blades?"

"If it wasn't for the stupid stupid *stupid* roller blades, I wouldn't have hurt Aunt Ellen."

"You didn't hurt Aunt Ellen, she just got sick all of a sudden and she happened to be wearing roller skates, Zin, that's all . . . and she's going to be all right."

"How do you know?"

"Because the doctor told me. She said Aunt Ellen's had a stroke, but that she's a strong woman and there's a good chance of her getting better. So there."

"I don't even know what a stroke is."

"That's what happens when a little tiny blood vessel in your brain breaks. And when that happens, your brain doesn't work like it's supposed to. And sometimes it fixes itself, or the doctors can fix it . . . and sometimes . . ."

"And then she dies?"

"Zin, now listen. Nobody lives forever, but you have to try and believe she's going to be all right, okay? Because if you believe it, she'll believe it and that's really important. And in a few months she'll be fine — she'll be as good as new."

"No she won't, Daddy."

"Zin . . ."

"Why won't they let us see her?"

"The doctor thinks it's best that she be alone and quiet now."

"Well *why*? When I'm sick you're always beside me. Auntie Ellen doesn't have anyone to be beside her."

"The doctors and nurses are with her now. She'll be all right. So there. Now why don't you believe me?"

"Because you won't let me see her."

"Zin, it's not me, those are the rules here — hospital regulations — children aren't allowed into intensive care!"

"How come?"

"I don't know, Zin. That's just the way it is."

"But I want to see her! It's not fair that I can't see her!"

Dad put his face in his hands, then looked up at Zinny. His voice sounded flat and tired.

"She's not going to look very nice Zin . . . She can't move . . . She can't talk . . . She has tubes . . . attached . . . and machines. Her face might be yellow . . . And yes, she might die."

***

We are walking down a corridor, past rooms with people dying in them. We walk past the nurses' counter. One nurse is standing there studying a chart. She looks up as we pass. She doesn't say anything. She looks back at her chart. It's funny what you can get away with if you need to.

We go into Aunt Ellen's room. We know it's hers because the sign outside says, "Intensive Care Unit."

She is lying on a bed, just like Dad described. Her eyes are closed and the only reason we know she is alive is because of a monitor next to her. It is making beeping sounds with a red light blipping across a screen. The blipping light makes you want to stare, like the light *is* Aunt Ellen, like it has more meaning than a dead-looking old woman lying on the bed.

Zinny doesn't seem to notice this.

"Hi, Auntie," she whispers.

Aunt Ellen's eyes slowly open.

"Dad sneaked us in so we could say hi . . . so hi. Sorry I made you go roller skating with me."

"It wasn't your fault Zin, I'm sure Aunt Ellen knows that," says Dad.

"Well anyway, I'm sorry . . . Can you hear me?"

Aunt Ellen blinks her eyes, slowly, but you know that it means she can.

"Oh I'm glad. Glad you can hear me. Are you glad?"

Aunt Ellen blinks again. This time a tiny bit faster. And her mouth, the right side of her mouth is trying to move, to smile.

"I'm glad too, Ellen," says Dad.

"Me too," I say. I've got a lump in my throat as big as a bird.

"Dad says you're going to be all right — that the doctor said ... Oh, and I thought of an excellent new tongue twister for you — *I* can hardly say it slow! Do you want to hear it? Maybe I should practice first, but I could tell you anyway ..."

But Zinny stops because right now Aunt Ellen's eyes are opening wider and there's tears in them.

"What's the matter, Aunt Ellen?" says Zin. She turns to Dad. "Dad?"

"Aunt Ellen needs lots of rest right now, Zin. We can come back tomorrow and you can tell her then, okay?" Then Dad turns to Aunt Ellen. "We better go now — sneak back out before we get caught. We're pulling for you, Ellen." He leans over and kisses her on the cheek. "You guys say good-bye now."

But before we can say anything, we watch as Aunt Ellen's lopsided lips slowly open and we listen as she barely whispers two words.

"To-oy Bo-oat."

===O=== **The Blue Camaro**

My sister came out of her room this morning and announced that she was leaving home. She's not leaving today or tomorrow, but in the fall when she'll be going to some big deal music school someplace down in the States. This is typical of her. She plans her life like a piece of music. She rehearses it and rehearses it till she gets it right. Then she plays it in public.

I wish I could be like that. I just crash ahead from moment to moment, and I never know what's coming next. Dad says I'm like my Uncle Jake. He says it like he wishes I wasn't, but I don't mind at all.

You got to know my Uncle Jake. He works down south in the oil patch. He runs a service company that takes care of oil wells or natural gas or something. Anyway, I don't see him often, but when he comes up here to visit, it's always an interesting time. Sometimes, too interesting.

He gets these phone calls when he visits us. They're from his partner, Ron, who calls at all hours of the day or night.

Dad will pick up the phone and say, "It's Ron," and Uncle Jake will take the call in another room. Dad sort of looks at Mom and shrugs his eyebrows.

My Dad and Uncle Jake are brothers. My Dad has a couple of university degrees. Uncle Jake's got grade ten.

The differences don't end there.

Dad drinks a little wine. Uncle Jake drinks a lot of beer.

Dad jogs and plays squash. Uncle Jake smokes and plays hockey.

Dad has a Volvo. Uncle Jake has a blue Camaro.

And we never visit Uncle Jake. Uncle Jake visits us. Dad says it's because he lives in a trailer and doesn't have room. About the only thing they have in common is their last name, Unruh — that and music; they both play guitar. I mean they don't like the same kind of music but it doesn't seem to bother them. They take turns playing the kind they like, while the other sort of plays along. So do I.

Mom wanted me to take classical guitar like my sister, Jana. I took up the bass instead. I figured it would be easier because a bass only has four strings, but after I got into it, I found out that it was probably as hard as the guitar. The only difference is that you can make a lot more mistakes on a bass and nobody will notice.

Except Jana, the classic loner.

When it comes to music, nobody knows more. But when it comes to other stuff, nobody knows less. "Get a life," I tell her, but all she does is look at me like I'm cheese mould. Even though we're less than two years apart, Jana and I might as well live in different cities. And I guess pretty soon we will. She's always been the brainy one who never gets in trouble, the one who looks away when I do get in trouble. She had a boyfriend, Chuck, and she went out with him every night for about three months. Then, boom, something happened. No more Chuck. And she started to live in her room with her guitar. I gave her this stuffed rabbit I have, trying to cheer her up. It's kind of a family joke but she never laughed.

About once or twice a year, Dad and Uncle Jake gather themselves into the rec room with a case of beer and a bottle of wine. And even though our house is a "no smoking zone", the rule kind of gets tossed out the window when they unpack their guitars, position a couple of chairs in the middle of the room and play till two or three in the morning.

Dad sings old Beatle tunes and other hits from the sixties. He doesn't have a bad voice, but he sings in keys that are too high which makes him sound squeezed and shrill.

Uncle Jake doesn't really sing at all. He kind of talks these country-and-western songs about broken hearts and truck drivers. He has a cigarette hanging out of his mouth and can make his voice go really low. I think his favorite song is "Me and Bobby McGee".

Last year I joined them for the first time, as a player, playing more wrong notes than right ones. Things haven't changed much in a year. I sit here, tonight, trying to keep up with my bass, afraid to ask anything, like what key we're in, or if Bobby McGee is a guy or a girl. It doesn't matter anyway. I am here, being a part of it.

Jana never joins.

Halfway through the night, the music will gradually fade and they'll start telling stories about when they were younger.

Last year Dad told one about when he was a university student and although I don't usually remember these stories, this one sticks in my mind because I can't imagine my Dad doing stuff like this. It makes you think twice about your parents and the kind of people they were in the sixties — parading around the street with protest signs against the war. Dad doing this, wearing sandals.

At the university, the engineers were the ones who were always pulling off these student pranks and getting into trouble with the campus cops. Anyway, my dad and a couple of his buddies had this neat idea to test out how wars start. Their theory was that if two groups of people are *not* who they *think* they are, they will *fight* to find out. So this is what they did.

Apparently there was a maintenance crew, digging up a road on the campus. The road happened to be right next to the Engineering Building. So Dad and his buddies went up to the road crew and warned them that *that* day was "dress up day" and they should look out for a bunch of engineering students dressed up like campus cops.

Then they wandered over to the campus cops and told the cops that there were a bunch of engineering students over by the Engineering Building pretending to be a maintenance crew digging up the road — digging a tunnel to the girls' residence.

They did all this with very straight faces. Then they sat back behind some bushes and watched.

Sure enough, war broke out.

But what happened is that Dad and his buddies were laughing so hard, that one of the campus cops saw them and before they knew it, there were half a dozen cops plus the entire road crew chasing them. They managed to hide out in the basement of the library but got locked in overnight. In the end, they were caught, not for seeing how wars start, but for being in the library overnight.

Uncle Jake laughed and said, "Yeah, everybody is an outlaw, just waiting to get caught," and he laughed some more.

So this is the kind of stories they tell and tonight will be no different.

Uncle Jake is halfway through singing "Me and Bobby McGee" when he breaks a string. He doesn't stop though — he keeps singing right to the end. I don't know if you know the song, but it has about a half-hour of "la-la's" in the final chorus, "la-la's" and the name, Bobby McGee. It always struck me as a kind of waste of time, like somebody was too lazy to figure out what words to write, so they put in "la-la's" instead.

While Uncle Jake is putting a new string on his guitar and Dad has gone to the bathroom, I actually say this. I say this stuff about the "la-la's".

Uncle Jake looks at me. He takes the cigarette out of his mouth and he says, "Oh no, those are the words. You just got to figure out what they mean." And he winks at me. I hate it when people wink. Like you're supposed to know something you don't.

Dad comes back in the room, "Oh," he says, "did you hear Josie got a new car." Josie is my aunt, my mom's sister, the family wacko. She used to be a Buddhist monk but now she's into real estate. "She bought a Porsche," Dad says.

"Oh yeah?" says Uncle Jake.

"Yeah, she doesn't drive it though. She keeps it locked in her garage."

"Locks are for honest people," says Uncle Jake. "If a *thief* wants something, he'll bugger the lock and take it. A buddy of mine did the same thing."

Here I know there's a story coming. They usually start like this. Uncle Jake puts the guitar down and takes a sip of beer.

"He buys a new Camaro, a brand spanking new blue Camaro, just like mine, same year and everything. Except his is not off the lot. He gets his special ordered, with all the bells and whistles, loaded. It's been triple lacquered, power this, remote that — it's got enough horses to launch the shuttle. The passenger seat turns into a living room couch. Plus he sinks another three grand into a stereo just to make your ears bleed. I mean it's got *everything*. The rubber alone'll set you back a couple a month's rent."

Here he takes another sip of beer, to wet his tongue and pause for dramatic effect.

"So he's got this zillion dollar car, *and he's afraid to drive it.* I mean, what if somebody should *breathe* on it or something? But not only is he afraid to *drive* it, he's afraid to *park* it. The guy is beside himself. He stays up at night with a shotgun protecting his car and the car is locked in his garage. He's losing sleep. During the day, he has his wife check on the car every twenty minutes.

"But because he's losing sleep at night, he's falling asleep at work during the day. If he doesn't smarten up, he's going to lose his job and not be able to make payments on his car.

"So he buys a dog. A great big jeez German shepherd watchdog. This's going to solve his problems. Everybody's going to be happy — him, his wife, his boss. But the stupid dog pees on one of his million dollar tires, so he shoots the dog. Honest-to-god, this is the truth," says Uncle Jake.

Dad is sort of snickering. Uncle Jake takes another sip of beer.

"The guy buys a couple grand worth of hi-tech, tamper-proof security equipment. It's hooked right into the police station. If anybody *looks* at his friggin' car, the cops'll be there in a minute and a half. So he figures he's pretty safe, the car's pretty safe.

"But all of a sudden, his mother dies. She just drops dead out of the blue. No warning, nothing. Trouble is, his mother lives in Edmonton, and it's a fifteen-hour drive there. So now he's got to decide if he's going to take his car or not. But his tamper-proof security system isn't much good hooked up to the police station in Estevan when the car's in Edmonton. So he parks the car carefully, nose into his garage, all hooked up to the security system and takes a bus to Edmonton. He gets to Edmonton . . . "

The phone rings. Dad answers. "It's Ron," says Dad. It's about half-past midnight.

"I'll take it upstairs," says Uncle Jake. He bolts up the stairs.

Dad waits till he can hear voices, then he hangs up the phone. He looks at me and shrugs his eyebrows. This is the look he usually gives to Mom, but she's in bed.

"Who is Ron anyways?" I ask.

"I don't know," says Dad. "We've never been introduced."
He picks up his guitar and strums a few chords.

"He picks a fine time to call," I say.

"Yeah, we're just getting to the good part," says Dad.

"How do you know?"

"Well I know the story," says Dad.

"You do?"

"*Everybody* knows the story," he says.

"Well *I* don't," I say. I'm a little annoyed that Dad knows
how this is going to end.

"It's *apocryphal*," says Dad. He uses these big words and I
don't know what they mean. Usually he explains them, like
he does right now. "It's one of these things you hear about,
but you doubt they ever happened. The trick is making it
sound new."

"So then what happens?"

"I'm not going to tell you. Let Jake tell you."

"That's 'cause you don't know," I say, taunting a little.

"No, I just don't want to wreck his story."

"Yeah, sure." He doesn't know any more about it than
I do.

"I'll give you a hint," he says. "It ends with a note on the
windshield."

"Yeah?" Now I'm really irritated. "So why's he bother
telling it then?"

"Well, you don't know how it's going to end, do you?"

"No."

"It's not what the *story* says, it's what it says about the
person who's telling it. It's like my story about what starts wars.
That's apocryphal too."

"It never happened?"

"Of course not. What kind of guy do you think I am?"

"So how come you tell it then?"

"Because I like it. It's the kind of guy I wish I was."

"Well *I* tell it because I think it's true."

"That's the kind of guy you wish I was too." He smiles at me.

If this was a movie, the camera would fix on my face right now, and there wouldn't be any expression on it. But you would know, that I would know, that he was right. Then the scene would change to Uncle Jake bounding down the stairs.

But this isn't a movie and I'm sitting there with a bass in my lap, and it's suddenly like a two-by-four, a piece of lumber with strings on it that's supposed to be a musical instrument. I'm in the basement, in the rec room with these guys, these two men, my uncle and my dad, and they're telling stories to each other that aren't true.

I don't know why it hits me right now, but everything you know is pretty well made up of stories people tell you. And if they're not true, then what's the point of telling them? What is true? How can you *know* anything?

"So-o-o!" says Uncle Jake, bounding down the stairs. "Where was I?"

"Mom's dead, car's in the garage," Dad says.

"Oh yeah. So he takes the bus to Edmonton, leaves his car nose in in the garage at home, locked up tighter than a can of sardines, with all the security stuff turned on, and he's gone for three days. Buries his mother and comes back home. He and his wife get out of the cab they took from the bus depot but before he goes into the house, he wants to check the car in the garage.

"He turns off the security system.

"And there it is — perfect. His shiny new Camaro. But — his jaw drops, he turns white. The car has been turned around! The front is now facing out! And right there, stuck under the wiper blade, on the windshield, is a note."

Here, I look at Dad. He smiles. Uncle Jake continues.

"He takes the note. He reads it. It says, 'If we really want it, Bud, we'll take it.'"

Dad laughs. Uncle Jake laughs. "So, Li'll Buddy, *you* got any stories?" he says to me.

"No," I say.

"Your rabbit died," says Dad.

"Oh yeah, my rabbit died."

"Yeah?" says Uncle Jake. "And then what?"

"Dad buried him and we went to the lake and when we came home, he was back in the hutch."

"He was alive?"

"No, he was dead. It looked like he was eating a carrot, but he was dead."

"Well that's a good story," says Uncle Jake. He laughs.

"Yeah but it's true," I say, getting up. "How can it be good?" I head towards the stairs and start climbing. I don't know why I'm leaving, but I am.

"What's wrong with him?" I hear Uncle Jake ask. Dad says something about hormones. I don't bother listening.

I'm still carrying my stupid bass without even realizing it so I go down the hall to put it in my room. I can hear Jana playing her guitar. I pause for a moment, hearing how good she really is. I wish I could join her. Instead, I cross back through the kitchen and go outside.

It's cool, but clear. The snow is just about gone. The sky is like a humungous warped blackboard, full of tiny silver holes. Uncle Jake's Camaro is in the driveway. He must have backed it in, because it's facing the street. I try the door. It's open. I get in. *Locks are for honest people,* Uncle Jake said.

The keys are in the ignition.

I shiver, not from cold but from a sudden feeling of power, sitting there, knowing you can take this thing right now and drive anywhere in North America. I get this idea that I should turn the car around, facing the other way, and then leave a note in the windshield. *Way deep down, everybody is an outlaw.* He said that too.

I turn the ignition key. The car growls to life.

A pair of headlights appear down the street. They stop. I wait for them to park. I don't want to do this with any traffic around. But the headlights move again — they approach. I can see now they belong to a car. It drives by, crunching on the half-frozen street.

It's a cop car.

My heart rushes. I wait for it to be well out of sight, even though the Camaro is rumbling low and impatient. I carefully slip the shift into drive. There is a solid clunk and the Camaro lunges ahead. I jam on the brake.

I didn't even have my foot on the gas.

I decide that this is not a good idea. I want to just turn the thing off and go back into the house, except that I'm half-way across the sidewalk. I'm afraid to put it in reverse because it might jump backwards through the garage door and all the way into the kitchen before I find the brake again. So I edge ahead and turn onto the street.

I stop. Now I can back up without worrying about exploding through the garage. I turn to look behind me.

Another set of headlights are bearing down fast! Maybe it's the cop.

Thinking fast, I figure my best bet is to keep on going forward, around the block, then straight into the driveway. This is what I'm going to do. I nose ahead, hardly moving. I feel like I'm at the helm of the *Starship Enterprise*, about to go into warp drive. But something is wrong. I check the instrument panel.

No lights!

I am now driving down the street with a car right behind me and I don't have any lights. I don't know how fast I'm going. The corner is coming up. I'm frantically fumbling for the light switch. Suddenly the windshield is all blurry, I'm blind. The wipers come on. I can see again. I've hit the wrong switch and cleaned the windshield. I'm at the corner.

With one hand I crank the steering wheel, the other is still looking for the light switch. I find another knob. I pull it. Light fills the street as well as the dashboard behind the wheel. Yes!

And there, looming right in front of me, fully awash in my new found headlights, is a parked truck. I've turned the corner too wide. I go to jam on the brakes. I miss. I hit the gas.

The moment of impact is like everything you've ever heard. It's all in slow motion. You actually have time to think. And you remember the thoughts you have in that moment. I have two of them: "Boy, am I in trouble," and "Why did I do this?"

Then, crunch.

It is a few seconds later. I am still sitting behind the steering wheel. My arms are sore. The lights are still on and the car is still running. There is a spider-web crack high on the clean windshield. My forehead throbs.

I open the car door. The interior light comes on. My plan is to go outside and inspect the damage, to do something about what has just happened. But I don't. I sit there stunned, staring at the car floor.

The impact of the collision has thrown everything that was under the seat out onto the floor. There are some tools, a wrench, a can of WD-40 and two magazines.

It is the magazines that I am looking at. Their covers have men on them, men in bathing suits. I pick one up. I open it. There are more pictures of men. They don't have any clothes on. They are doing things with their bodies for the camera. Picture after picture. I close the magazine and quickly shove both of them back under the seat.

***

After the police come and take me to the hospital, where they x-ray me and bandage my head, my parents arrive. Uncle Jake is not with them. The look on their faces tells me they're glad I'm all right. Mom hugs me, but Dad doesn't. He doesn't want to give me the impression that he approves of what I did. It is now about three-thirty in the morning.

In the car, driving home, Dad asks me why I did it, why I took Uncle Jake's car. I tell him I was just going to turn it around in the driveway and put a note on the windshield. That I just meant it as a joke.

"It's not very funny though, is it?" he says.

"No," I say.

"You're going to have to pay for it, you know — all the damage."

"I know." There is a pause here, while Dad is thinking of how I'm going to pay for this. But that is not what I'm thinking, not at all. I'm thinking of those magazines on the floor of the car. I am thinking of them and Uncle Jake.

"Where's Uncle Jake?" I ask.

"He's home, sleeping. He has to get back to Estevan tomorrow. He's going to have to take a bus."

"He's not very pleased, you know," says Mom.

It's right now that I start crying. I can't help it. The tears just start flooding out of my eyes and I feel stupid, and mad that I can't stop. I bang the back seat with my fist.

"It's okay, dear, it's okay," says Mom.

"No it's not," I say and I want to tell them about the magazines. I want to ask them about Uncle Jake and why he has them. I want to know who Ron is. I want to know why we sit in the basement and sing songs and tell stupid stories that don't mean anything. I want to know this. And this is why I'm crying. It's because I'm so stupid that I'm crying, because I don't know anything that I'm crying, and because I don't know how to find out that I'm crying.

"Calm down!" says Dad. "It's not the end of the world."

I stop banging the seat.

It's not far from the hospital to our place, so I'm still a snivelling idiot when we get there.

Sitting in the living room is Uncle Jake and when we enter, he gets up and comes to me. I can't look him in the eyes. He puts his arm around my shoulder and says, "It's okay, Buddy. It's okay."

I shake his arm off and run down the hall to my room.

I'm sitting on my bed thinking about how rotten I'm feeling, when there's a soft knock on my door. I don't want to see anybody. Especially Uncle Jake.

"Go away," I say.

"It's me," whispers Jana.

This surprises me. However, I don't say anything. She takes this as permission to enter. It is.

She comes in and sits down at the edge of my bed. It's dark. I expect her to say something. But she just sits there, quiet. It's me who breaks the silence.

"Yeah?" I say.

"Are you okay?" she asks.

"Yeah." I lie. "I'm okay."

She reaches out and puts her hand on my foot. I can't recall her ever touching me before, willingly. She gives my foot a little squeeze, then removes her hand completely. "Okay," she says, and gets up to leave.

I suddenly realize I don't want her to go. I want her to stay there and be with me a little while. I don't want to be alone.

"What do you do when you find out something, and you don't know how to tell people?"

Jana sits down again. "I don't know," she says. "I usually just cry. Or play guitar."

"You were playing tonight," I say.

"I play every night." There is a pause here, while we try to figure out what to say next. We're not used to talking. "Thanks for the rabbit," she says.

"What rabbit?" Then I remember the stuffed rabbit I gave her when she broke up with Chuck. "Yeah, well you were pretty depressed."

"I meant to thank you sooner, but . . . "

"What?"

"The time just never seemed right."

"So how come it's right now?"

"I don't know. It just *is*."

I've never seen my sister like this before, even though it's dark and I can't see her at all. I've never thought of her as feeling the same way I do. And at that moment, we do feel the same and I know it. But I don't know how to tell her that.

"I like you Jana."

"I like you too," she says, and gives my foot another squeeze.

"You know what we should do?" I want to share this time with Jana.

"What?"

"We should go and play some tunes together."

"Yeah, we should."

And here there is another pause, like we're imagining how this could actually happen. Then quietly, out of the black, Jana asks the oddest question:

"Did you know that Aunt Josie bought a Porsche? She keeps it locked in her garage."

It's like a cue, like something we rehearsed. And I know the answer.

"Locks are for honest people," I say. "If a thief really wants it, he'll figure out a way to get it."

"Yeah," Jana chuckles.

"It reminds me of this friend of a *friend of mine*," I continue, "who bought a new Camaro, it's blue, like Uncle Jake's, except it's triple lacquered and this thing is *loaded* ... "

We tell stories the rest of the night. We tell secrets.

Kurt's Mom's Funeral

I stopped laughing when the cops arrived. It was Kurt who kicked over the gravestone. The cops are asking me what I know. I'm not sure what I'll tell them because Kurt and I are friends. Even though we're opposites, we've been friends ever since I can remember.

Kurt's parents would be in their sixties if they were both still alive. He has a brother and a sister who are much older than he is. Kurt was "an accident", like me. We're both seventeen. Our parents are practically the same age as most people's grandparents. We both have nieces and nephews who are older than us. It's really stupid.

When we were little, Kurt used to come over and play at my house all the time. That's because he wasn't allowed to bring people over to his house, even before his mom died. His mom hated any kind of dirt. She used to have plastic covers on all their furniture and would run around dusting and cleaning all day long. Except when she was sick, which was a lot of the time. And Kurt hated it because he would have to go home and do stuff he didn't want to do because his dad said.

Even though I wasn't allowed in their house to play, I was in their bathroom once *because I had to go and couldn't hold it* and it was like going in a drugstore, for all the bottles and pills. Mostly I was made to stand at the back door and wait while Kurt got his boots on or whatever. Their house had a strange sour smell, like dirty socks. But there were sure never any socks lying around.

Kurt is a tall, very good looking guy with blond hair and blue eyes. I've seen girls bump into things watching him walk down the hall at school. He plays junior B hockey and is a star on the ball team too. I'm sort of the opposite. I'm not that big, and I'm sure not good looking, and I'm lousy at sports. Girls don't know I exist.

The only thing I'm half-good at, is school. Or at least I used to be, which is why I went to so many funerals. I was an altar boy and whenever somebody died and Father Boyd needed someone to serve at the funeral mass, he'd call me. He knew I could miss a couple of hours of school and it wouldn't cause me to flunk out, like it would some people, like Kurt. So I got to know funerals, all kinds.

When you go to a lot of them, you stop feeling sorry for people who died and you pay more attention to those who are still alive and their different ways of being sad. The funerals with the biggest sorrows were the ones with the tiniest coffins.

The most interesting ones were where the women would wail and weep in some foreign language and throw themselves onto the coffin as it was being lowered into the ground.

I saw that happen twice and both times it seemed fake, like it was acting, like this is what the woman was supposed to do, a weird ritual of some kind. And maybe it was, because Father Boyd would never skip a beat. He'd just roll along, sprinkling holy water and saying holy words while two or three men would try to haul the woman from on top of the coffin and she'd be clutching it with all her might. You wondered for a minute if they'd get her off before they started shovelling on the dirt. They always did.

After a while the funerals started being the same and I grew to understand why Father Boyd never missed a beat no matter what. He just wanted to get the thing over with, so he could do whatever else he was supposed to do and get away from these stupid boring death scenes with people crying and all dressed in black, and someone always propping some old woman up, like getting her ready because she's probably the next one to go.

So when Kurt's mom died, it was a shock because of all the funerals I had been at, and I had served thirty or forty by the time I was thirteen, I had never personally known anyone who was being buried. I remember too that there was some question as to whether or not there should be a funeral mass. When this is a question it means one thing. It means that suicide is suspected. And because suicide is a sin, it means you can't have a mass. But Father Boyd always gave the benefit of the doubt to people. *Judge not, lest you yourself be judged,* he would say, and Kurt's mother's funeral had a mass.

I don't know how many people knew about this, but I knew about it and when I saw Kurt before the funeral he said she got her pills mixed up and that's what killed her. Then he looked at me and sort of smiled, just for an instant, a terrible, awful smile. Maybe he smiled because he didn't know what else to do, or maybe because he was glad she was dead and was embarrassed for feeling like that. I don't know.

Anyway, I'm serving the mass at Kurt's mother's funeral and Kurt and his father are sitting in the front pew next to the coffin. Kurt's father is looking very solemn with his eyes fixed on the floor, and Kurt is looking exactly the same. Kurt's older brother and sister are there too, with Kurt's nieces and nephews that are older than him, all sitting there dressed in black and looking all very solemn.

When all of a sudden Kurt looks up and just for a second our eyes meet. And just as quickly as he had looked up, he looks away and back down again. But I can see his mouth is doing something strange, that he is tightening the muscles around his lips. That he is trying not to smile at me.

As soon as I realize that he is trying not to smile, it has an amazing effect on me. It makes me try not to smile too. And the harder I try not to smile, the more I want to. If I look up and see Kurt, and Kurt is still trying not to smile as well, I know what will happen, that not only will I smile, I will laugh. Out loud. So now, I am not only trying not to smile, I am trying not to look at Kurt. This should be an easy thing to do. If I *decide* not to look at Kurt, I *will* not look at him and nothing in heaven or hell should be able to *make* me look at him. But if I don't look at him, I won't know if he is trying not to smile or not. So I look.

Kurt is no longer trying not to smile. He *is* smiling.

I start laughing. I can't help it. I turn away and want to bury my head in my surplice. I am snorting and jiggling. It's like someone has dumped a bag of marbles on a hardwood floor and they are bouncing and rolling in a million directions and I don't know how to stop them. I know they shouldn't be there. They belong in their bag. Except these marbles are laughs and they are rolling throughout the church and they belong to Kurt and me.

It is now that Father Boyd looks at me and the look he gives me says, "What the hell are you doing?" Except that it is so exaggerated that it makes me laugh even harder and I do the only sane thing I can think of. I run away. I run to the sacristy. I sit on a chair in the sacristy and I laugh till tears run down my face. I am laughing at Kurt's mother's funeral and I don't know why.

It is the last time I serve at a funeral.

***

I didn't have many friends at school aside from Kurt. He always gave me stuff, automatically shared what he had with me, even though I never had the same kinds of things to share back. It never seemed to bother him and it never bothered me either, except once.

It was late spring the year before the funeral and about a dozen of us were playing scrub baseball in the school yard. The far end of the yard was overgrown in wild oats and thick grass because there'd been a lot of rain and the mowers were behind in their cutting.

We were using Kurt's ball and bat because he has the knack of getting such things even though his dad doesn't buy them for him. Kurt will hang around when the big guys are playing and eventually he will find something they have left or misplaced and he will claim it as his own. It is not really stealing, he tells me. "It's *finding*. You just have to know where to look." Kurt always knows where to look. He got most of his hockey equipment that way too.

I was playing in left field where it was furthest out of the way and where I would do less damage than on the infield. Kurt was pitching. This was fair because not only was Kurt the best player and the best player always pitches, but it was his ball. However, Kurt didn't have his usual stuff that day and Franky cracked one high over my head.

I ran and stumbled backwards till I was practically waist high in the tall grass. This was where the ball had fallen. I looked and looked but I couldn't find the ball. Finally our whole team joined me, then theirs, and both teams were combing the tall grass, flattening it out till it looked like it'd been hit by a hail storm. Still no ball.

Eventually we went to resume the game with a second ball. Its seams were rotted, it was hard as a rock and it weighed a ton because it had been left in the rain too many times, then dried by the sun.

But before we began, Kurt said to me, "You got to get me a new one." It was as simple as that — I lost it — I replace it. I was responsible for replacing the lost ball, even though Kurt was the one who threw the bad pitch and Franky was the one who hit it into the grass. It didn't even occur to me to ask, "Why me?" I knew why. It went missing in my territory. I was in charge.

The baseball I lost was practically new. Parts of the cover were still unscuffed. And it was a good one too, one used by the big guys who wear uniforms even when they're practising. I knew that I would have to replace it with one that was just as good, one that cost a lot of money, a lot of money that I didn't have.

I would have to steal a baseball.

So while the game was still on, I took my bike to Canadian Tire but I didn't lock it like I usually did. This was so when I exited from the store with my stolen baseball I wouldn't have to tangle with my lock. I would be able to make a fast getaway. If somebody had stolen my bike while I was inside stealing a baseball, I would have understood.

I went inside the store. I had never stolen anything before, except maybe for a couple of chocolate bars, and I was surprised at how calm and cool I was. I walked into the sports section, to where they kept the baseballs, and I looked at the most expensive ones. They were wrapped in cellophane. I picked one up. It made a crinkling sound in my hand. I was about to put it into my pocket when a salesclerk walked down the aisle towards me.

"Can I help you?" he said to me.

"No," I said, "Just looking." And I flipped the ball a couple of times in my hand.

The clerk walked away, but just as he turned the corner around the end of the aisle, he glanced back at me. He knows, I thought to myself.

It was at that moment that I fully realized what I was doing. It didn't bother me that what I was doing was a sin, that I would have to go to confession and tell Father Boyd what I had done, and that he would give a penance of maybe a whole rosary and make me promise to make restitution. It didn't bother me that if I got caught, the store manager would call the police or my parents or maybe both and I would be in deep, big-time trouble. What bothered me is that I was stealing a baseball for Kurt. And that if I did not steal this baseball for Kurt, we would no longer be friends.

I slipped the cellophane-covered baseball into my pocket and walked out of the store.

Before I got half-way back to the school yard, I stopped at a boulevard. I took the cellophane off the ball and I rubbed it in some dirt and clumps of grass. I tried to make it look like the one I lost. All this had taken twenty minutes.

When I gave the ball to Kurt, he looked at it, exchanged it with the old one in his glove, then threw the old one against the backstop. And continued the game. He didn't say a word to me.

I went back out to left field.

I played very deep. I was on the edge of the tall grass. I did not want another ball to go over my head. Suddenly I stepped on something that almost turned my ankle. I looked down, and there was Kurt's first ball. I picked it up and put it into my pocket. I felt my face burning and stupid angry tears coming into my eyes. I was standing there in left field crying and I didn't know why.

★★★

Dad works at the mine. He's a supervisor there, but he's going to retire next year. Kurt's dad worked there too, but he got hurt and he's been on disability pension. It happened just after Kurt's mom died.

Kurt has just got his driver's license and because of his dad's bad back, Kurt gets the car just about any time he wants it. I'm not sure he asks for it, I get the feeling he just takes it. Anyway, a bunch of us are in the car and we're cruising around because there is nothing else to do. We'll end up at the mall parking lot where everyone else will stop and park too. We all hang out there talking and horsing around, hoping to find out there's a party or something else going on. Sometimes the cops come and check for booze and tell us to leave even though they know there's nowhere for us to go. That's what it's usually like, but some nights are different.

Tonight we pull into the lot and there's already a row of cars and trucks parked facing the main street. I recognize a bunch of people including a girl named Shawna I'd like to meet. Kurt says he'll introduce me if I behave myself. It's his way of joking and at the same time reminding me that he knows everyone in town.

We park next to a battered black half-ton bush-truck with roll bars and boom-boxes blasting heavy metal. Three guys are sitting in the truck-box, nodding in time to the music. We don't know them. One of them is wearing a black baseball cap that says, *Eat Shit.*

I'm kind of excited about the possibility of meeting Shawna and in my rush to get out of the car, I swing the door wide open — too wide open. I hit the side of the pickup.

The three guys pop out of the box like they are spring-loaded. Eat Shit is running his hand over the side panel like he's feeling for a dent or scrape, except the truck is full of them.

"Sorry," I say, "It was an accident."

"It was an accident, eh! Well this was an accident too," the guy says and kicks the side of Kurt's dad's car. "You're going to pay for this."

"For what, which one?" I ask, referring to all the scrapes.

"What's the matter, you blind?"

He grabs my shoulder and swings me face-first into the side of his truck. My forehead slams against the door.

"There! Now can you see it? Can you see it now, pizza face?" He grinds my nose against the scarred, black paint.

'Leave him alone, Shithead," says Kurt. He grabs the guy's hat. "Oh, is this your name, or just something you like to do?"

The guy's grip on me relaxes.

"Gimme back my hat," he says to Kurt.

But before he can actually move from me, I turn in time to see Kurt flash a quick boot into the guy's crotch. He crumples to the ground. Kurt then kicks him in the head. Twice. The sound is sickening. No one moves.

"You eat shit," says Kurt. He turns and walks around the car to the driver's side. We all scramble in.

As we pull away, we see two figures hunched over a third. They are trying to get him up.

There is silence in the car. No one wants to talk. The passing street lights alternate a half-shade, then glare across Kurt's stone face. It was all so quick, it's almost like it didn't happen. But I am still shaking. The sound of Kurt's boots thucking against the side of Eat Shit's skull still echoes through my own.

Very slowly, imperceptibly, Kurt starts rocking back and forth. And as his rocking increases in depth and intensity, so does the speed of the car. Finally, the silence breaks. Frank is the first to speak.

"What are you doing, Kurt?"

"Hey man, you're doing eighty!"

"Slow down!"

"Come on, Kurt! Slow down!"

"Watch that light! You're going to go through that light!"

At the last moment Kurt jams on the brakes. The car screams to a halt. A pause.

"Okay, you wanted me to stop. I stopped. Now shut up."

Once again everyone is quiet. It seems that Kurt is calmed. He is driving slowly now and turns down the street of our old school. It looks small in the dark and it once seemed so big. For eight years it was the biggest building in our lives, that and the church. Kurt pulls up beside the ball field. He leaves the car running.

"I know," says Kurt. "Let's go look for baseballs."

"What?" somebody in the back seat asks.

"Mark lost one here once, and we never did find it, did we, Mark?"

I hesitate.

"No," I say. "I don't think so."

This makes Kurt chuckle. He slaps the steering wheel a couple of times with the palm of his hand.

"You know the trouble with you, Marky, is you've always been such a shitty liar," Kurt says. He puts the car in gear. "You cry easy, but you're a shitty liar."

No one in the car knows what Kurt is talking about. Even I'm not totally sure and an uncertain silence once again joins the dark in Kurt's dad's car.

He turns onto a road heading out of town. The feeling of uncertainty grows.

"Where we going?" asks Frank from the back.

"To hell," says Kurt. A small smile on his face.

"No, really, where we going? I have to be home early tonight."

"You want to walk?" Kurt slows down, as though he is going to stop.

"No."

"Franky knows how to lie, Mark. He really would like me to stop right now so he could walk home. But he's afraid of what everyone will think, so he says no. Isn't that right, Franky?"

"No," says Frank, "If I want to walk, I'll walk."

"He's really good at it, Marky. So how come you never told me you found the ball?"

"I don't know." And I don't know why this is so important right *now*.

"You didn't have to steal one you know," says Kurt. "It was just a friggin' baseball." And he starts the slow rocking again, but instead of going faster like he did earlier, he goes slower. The effect, however, is the same. We all tense. "You always make me feel sorry for you," he says.

No, I want to say, *that's how you make me feel about you*.

He goes slower and slower till he finally stops altogether. We're at the cemetery. Kurt doesn't move from behind the wheel. He is still clutching it and looking straight ahead as if he was driving, even though the car is going nowhere.

Nobody knows what to do.

"I don't live here *yet*," Frank tries to joke.

Kurt slowly turns and looks at him. "I do," he says. "You want to come in? Come on in. I'll introduce you to my mother."

"No, that's fine," says Frank.

"Come on, I insist," says Kurt. He jumps out and opens the back door of the car like a chauffeur, holding his arm to show the way. "Gentlemen?" he says.

They all get out of the back seat and stand there in the half-light, shuffling and nodding like prisoners at an execution. Kurt closes the door. He leans through the driver's window.

"Mark? Aren't you coming?"

"No, you go. I'll stay here."

"I want you to come, Mark."

"I don't want to go to a graveyard at midnight."

"I want you to come, Mark," he repeats.

"Why?"

"I don't want to be alone."

"You got company," I say. There's three of them standing there, wondering if he's the executioner.

"*But they've never been to my house,*" he says.

There is no argument against this and even though I don't want to go, I do, because I can't think of anything else that makes any sense.

We follow Kurt to the graveyard. No one says a word. No one knows why we are doing this, why we are following Kurt, but we are. We know the cops regularly patrol here, that if you want to get into trouble, this is the place to be. At midnight.

When we get to the gate, Kurt says, "This is the front door, gentlemen. Please, your shoes. My mother doesn't like mud getting tracked through the house."

We look at him, uncomprehending.

"Take off your shoes," he says.

We take off our shoes. Kurt still wears his.

"Please, gentlemen, this way."

We follow. Mincing our way in stockinged feet across the gravel road onto the lawn littered with fallen twigs from the elms overhead. Rows of gravestones look like banks of rotten teeth.

"This, gentlemen, is Mother's living room. Notice the white carpet. The cellophane-wrapped lamp shades. And the vinyl covers on the couch and chair." He stops. "And this is the kitchen. You'll notice the white cupboards, and yes, those large porcelain crocks are full of freshly made sauerkraut. Isn't that a lovely smell? Breath deep."

We all breath deep. The only smell is of fresh clay and the faint decay of flowers covered in dew. Our feet are wet.

The barefoot death tour continues. "And this is my parents' bedroom. We can't go in there, gentlemen. But we can listen. Can you hear?" He starts kicking a tombstone. The sound is not unlike the sound of him kicking Eat Shit's head. "Yes, what are they doing in there?" He kicks the stone near the top, again and again, till it loosens. He then pushes and pulls till it topples. It lays there. Kurt is breathing hard. "What do you think, eh Franky? What's going on?"

"I don't know." Frank is stunned.

"Come on, what do you think?"

"I don't know," he repeats.

"Well you got a goddamn *mind*, what do you *think?*"

Frank is withered by embarrassment. His eyes search us for help. We look down, our arms crossed.

"I don't think anything," Frank says finally.

"I believe you," says Kurt. "You never had a thought in your life. But Mark knows — Mark has thoughts, don't you, Mark?"

I don't say anything.

"Mark knows that right next to the bedroom is the bathroom, isn't that right, Mark?"

I nod my head.

"Let's show them the bathroom. See gentlemen, this here's the bathroom." Kurt moves a few steps and falls onto his knees. He's on his knees, his arms stretched out like he's holding the world. "And what is in the bathroom? What is the bathroom full of? Mark? Tell them."

"Bottles," I say.

"Bottles of what?"

"Pills."

"Pills! Full of pills!" says Kurt and he starts grabbing handfuls of grass. "Full of pills!" He jumps up at Frank and he starts stuffing the grass at Franky's mouth, into his mouth. "Eat it, Franky! Eat it!" he says.

Frank stumbles back with Kurt screaming on top of him, "Eat!" I rush over and pull at Kurt. He swings at me like a madman and catches me in the jaw. I go down. Everything blurs.

"Lights!" someone yells.

"Cops!"

Frank scrambles to his feet and sprints off into the dark with the other two. I am too stunned to do anything. Kurt comes to me. He kneels beside me.

"Sorry, I'm sorry," he says.

"It's okay," I say.

By now the lights of the cop car are twenty yards away. We hear doors open, "Freeze!" a voice yells in the dark. It's a funny feeling knowing someone is pointing a gun at you with their finger on the trigger.

"I am freezing," I say to Kurt. "And I'm wet too." I start uncontrollably giggling at my own joke.

But Kurt isn't laughing. Instead, there's tears in his eyes.

"You know what I always liked about you?" says Kurt. "I liked when you laughed at my mother's funeral."

This is when the cops arrive.

If you want to have fun these days you got to jump up and down on people's heads or go live in somebody's nose. Like, who needs it? You can't even have sex without worrying about your *thing* falling off.

And then there's school.

I don't have anything against school. Any idiot knows you got to get your grade twelve. School is like something you got to do sooner or later. Some of my best friends go to school — I just don't understand how they can do it. It's like eating yogurt. You know it's supposed to be good for you — you just wish it had some taste and would stop making you gag. You make one mistake and everyone's jumping down your throat with rulers and chalk and guidance counsellors. They're so damn sure of themselves. They know everything. Somebody should take schools and put some flavour in them, move them to the twenty-first century. Who needs to know about the Crimean War? Or some poem by a dead guy about a cat licking windows? Give me a break.

Anyway, I can't stand it, so I quit. As a result of quitting, I get kicked out of the house.

"We're not going to support a life-style where you just bum around," says Dad. "You got to do something."

Dad is a Doctor. He likes it when you call him that even though he doesn't heal people or fix them up. He teaches at the University — philosophy. This kills me. He lives in a world that he's made in his mind. It's filled with people like Descartes and Kant — these guys who were philosophers. Descartes was the one who said, "I think, therefore I am." Yeah, well, I fart, therefore I am.

Anyway, he wants me to do something with my life. I don't fit in his head.

"Like what?" I ask.

"I don't care. If you can't go to school, then you can get a job. Work. Those are the rules in this house if you want to live here. If you don't, get out."

There's other rules too, like no sex or drugs. It's funny how the rules thing works. I mean there's rules for me, but does he have any? No, he has a rack full of guns and every fall he turns into Mr. *Field and Stream,* the Big White Hunter. He goes after deer mostly and over the winter we eat a lot of venison. We eat it so he can kill it. It's one of the rules he's worked out in his head, to keep company with Descartes and Kant. You get really sick of it after a while. I bet the deer aren't too happy about it either.

So, fine. Those are his rules. I'm not going to argue. I have other places to stay. On the street, with all the other "shitheads, lowlife, and scum". That's what my dad calls them.

What he doesn't know is that they're friends, a kind of a club, like the Elks or Lions, without the fancy hats. We got a motto too — "Watch Out or Die Ugly." Some people come here to do the ugly part. Most come here because there's nowhere else to go.

The first thing you learn is how to protect yourself. There's some really crazy people around who got that way when someone tried to eat them when they were three, or they got so strung out they don't know where they are, or don't have enough brain cells working to know which way is back. That's how come I got a knife. I keep it tucked in my sleeve, along my forearm. I don't use it, but I want people to know I have it. It's like you're saying, "Don't mess with me. I would hurt you."

I got my name for a stupid thing I did once. I'll tell you about it to show what kind of space you can get your head into without even really trying. I was at a party where somebody snagged some cash, so we had lots of booze. It was pretty late and we were talking about what you had to do if you wanted to commit suicide and Roxy was saying she knew someone who cut their wrists across, like where your watch band is. Except I know you can't do it that way. You have to cut up and down along your arm so you really wreck your veins. And to prove it, I cut my wrist, across.

There was lots of blood but dying was not what I did, otherwise, my name would be "Dead," instead of "Cut". Roxy has kept her distance from me ever since.

The truth is, it takes a lot more than a cut to kill someone. That's why when you hear about somebody dying from fifty or sixty stab wounds, it's not that the murderer is trying to be particularly nasty or anything, he's just trying to finish the job he's started. So unless you get really lucky and go for the throat, it usually takes a whole lot to kill someone. Ask any knife murderer. Not that I did personally — I just read it somewhere.

I do a lot of reading. Reading and sleeping. I like Stephen King. You can sort of read and sleep at the same time. People in his books are always nuts. They do one stupid thing and it haunts them for the rest of their lives. Like me, one thing and I get called Cut from then on.

I'm not going to tell you where I get my money because mostly I just bum. But sometimes I sell things that friends give me or they leave lying around and don't really need. Hey, what are friends for? But when winter came, everyone scrambled to get under a roof and it got harder and harder to find places to stay. Now that winter's just about over, I've run out of friends and it's still too cold to sleep outside.

So that's why I'm going to see my folks. I'm broke and I'm hungry and I need a place to stay. I know there won't be any problem. There never is when I go back. They just want me to go to school or get a job. I mean, I understand their point of view, I just don't feel like doing it. I get a buzz in my head when I think about it. But I'll play along. I'll look in the paper. I'll even go out and put some job applications in. Who knows, I might even get a job. But there's not much around, and what can you do with only grade eleven? Like you can pump gas or work in a kitchen doing dishes for five bucks an hour. Big deal. Who needs it?

I do.

My parents' place is on the outskirts of town. I have a sister too, but she's married and has three kids. The only reason I'm telling you this is because I don't want you to think I come from a "broken home," or some stupid thing. I was never abused when I was a kid and the only thing that ever went wrong was my dog died when I was five. Sure, some old guy showed me his dork but I was just amazed at all the hair. Nothing happened. I have no idea why I am the way I am.

Maybe it's those things that do happen to you and you don't even know what they mean. Like this other old guy I knew when I was about twelve.

We used to cross the train bridge and he lived in a shack next to the dump down by the river, just on the other side of the Power Plant. We would sometimes go and throw rocks at his place to get him to chase us. Of course, he always did.

One day there were four of us skinny-dipping and horsing around in a river shallow between two sand bars, about a half a mile from the old man's shack, when all of a sudden we look up, and there he is, picking our clothes up and stuffing them under his arm. Then he just stands there laughing. He's big, the old guy, and he's wearing a coat even though it's the middle of summer. He's dirty too, like he's been at the dump all day picking garbage. He probably has.

"I got you now," he says. "I got you."

And he does. There isn't anything we can do but try to hide behind our hands and be terrified.

"What should I do with these?" he says, referring to our clothes. "I think I'll trade them."

"No, mister, you can't!" We yell in our shrill twelve-year old voices. We're almost in tears.

"Yeah, that's what I'm going to do. Trade them."

"How're we going to get home?" We're pleading, with visions of ourselves riding our bikes naked through town.

"I'll trade them for a promise," he says.

We listen.

"You promise not to throw rocks at my place, I'll give you your clothes back."

"Yeah, yeah, we promise."

"I don't believe you," he says.

"We *do*, we won't throw rocks, we promise mister!"

"Okay, then come and get them," and he turns and goes, except he's still got our clothes under his arm.

"Wait mister, our clothes!"

But he disappears into the bushes, heading towards his shack, with everything but our shoes. We put on our shoes and follow, half-crouching and yelling. He leaves a trail of shirts and underwear.

When we finally get there, we see four pairs of pants strung out on a clothes line attached to the shack. In front of the shack is an old car seat, and in front of that, a smouldering fire-pit. The old guy appears at the door with a cup of something steaming in his hand.

"Ah, visitors!" he says.

"We want our pants back," I say.

"Help yourself," he says. "Just remember what you traded them for."

We approach like four shy dogs, our tails between our legs.

He sits on the battered car seat. "It's not often I get visitors," he says. "Anybody want some tea?"

"No, just our pants." We are now pulling them down from the line and scrambling into them. My sneakers get caught in the legs. I lose my balance and fall. Sitting on the ground, I yank my pants off again, remove my sneakers and start over.

"Come on, hurry," somebody says.

Suddenly, he holds the cup in the air like he's toasting, except he's looking off into the bush. Then he makes the strangest sound I ever heard. It's like a grunting but there seems to be some meaning attached to it.

That's when the deer walks out of the bush, a beautiful white-tail doe, and right behind her, a little fawn. They walk straight over to the old guy. He takes something out of his pocket and gives it to the doe, then pats her nose. All the while he's doing this, he's murmuring something soft. The doe turns and looks at us, at me really, and just as suddenly as they came, they disappear back into the brush.

I am still sitting on the ground with my pants half-on.

The old guy looks over at us again. "Tea?" he asks.

"Yeah," I hear myself say.

"Yeah," I hear the others.

That was the first of our many visits that summer.

"Everything wants to be round." He said it like it was a rule or a law.

I agree with him. Things break down. They wear out. Crumble smooth. I mean, take sand or a pebbly beach. They started out as mountains. And look how round they're getting. The whole planet's getting round.

If you live in a city, it doesn't look that way. It looks the opposite because we build things — houses, office towers, strip malls. But everything we build makes a hole somewhere else, in a forest, a field or under the ground. Nowhere is there a part untouched by hands. Everything's been measured and marked. And malled.

If you live on the prairies, where I'm from, you might think that everything gets flat. And that's true too, but really it's the same thing. For example, there used to be hundreds of thousands of buffalo on the prairies. There's only a few thousand left. They shot them all. You know why? Not for their tongues, not for the buffalo coats, not for their bones, but for *belts*. Leather belts.

All the big factories were run by steam engines in those days, and the way they turned the machinery was with great long expanses of buffalohide belts sewn together. That's where all the buffalo went. It took two men a whole day to skin a buffalo. And when they had just about run out of buffalo, they discovered rubber, and had rubber tree plantations in the tropics to make the belts out of dead rubber trees instead of dead buffalo.

That's what the old guy said, then he disappeared too.

The next summer when we went back, the place was empty like no one had lived there for a long time. And he was gone. We had no idea where he went, or if he was dead or what.

Sometimes I want to disappear like the old guy.

I get on the bus downtown and flash the bus pass that I found. I won't say where I found it, so don't ask. I sit about half-way down, behind an old lady with lots of bags. I sit next to the aisle, leaving the window seat open. This is so no one will sit next to me. I really don't have to worry because the bus is more than half-empty. It's just about seven, after supper.

It's quickly getting dark. You'd think because of all the snow that light wouldn't die so easy. But it does. The streets are rutted in iron-hard ice and everyone who tries to cross them takes those funny hurried steps that people take in winter. They don't have faces. People in winter never do.

The bus rolls to its stops, picks up people, lets people off. We're getting near my parents' home. The old lady with lots of bags finally gets off. She smiles at me. I'm the only one left, me and the bus driver. We come to a corner where there's a 7 Eleven. The bus stops and the driver gets out. He runs into the 7 Eleven leaving the door open. He's getting a coffee or something.

This is when the wolf gets on. I kid you not. A wolf.

The wolf is big. It's about a meter high. And it's pure white. I know it is a wolf because it has yellow eyes. He pads half-way down the bus till he gets to me. In one slow-motion leap, he sits on the seat across from me.

I just about shit.

I don't know if you've ever had a wolf sit next to you on a bus, but I tell you what, it doesn't make you feel like dancing.

I always liked wolves, or the *idea* of wolves. They're beautiful animals. They're free to come and go as they please. They don't have enemies, except for us — humans, or whatever we are. I'd never seen one up close before. They have these deadly yellow eyes, like they know something you can't even dream about.

Dogs never have yellow eyes, unless they're crossbred with wolves.

So there's these deadly eyes staring at me across the aisle, aimed at me. I don't know what to do. I think maybe I should say something. I say the first thing that comes to mind.

"Good boy," I say.

The wolf doesn't make a sound. He just shows me his teeth. They are surprisingly white, like he brushes and flosses everyday. Except they're really big. "Oh grandma, what big teeth you have." I think about yelling for help. I can see the bus driver chatting at the counter. The wolf licks his lips. I decide to wait.

"Good boy," I say again.

This time the wolf not only shows his teeth, he growls. Not that I can actually hear it, I can feel it. It's like a double resonance in harmony with the bus's diesel.

For the first time in my life, I am truly afraid. I don't know what's going on. This is too weird. Maybe I'm hallucinating or something. I quickly raise my hand to rub my eyes.

This time I hear the growl. Very slowly I remove my hand from my eyes. I lower it to my left sleeve, where I keep my knife. If I can have it out in two seconds, he can have his teeth clamped around my throat in one. The question is, who will do more damage? I leave the knife alone. The growl continues.

It stops when the driver steps on board the bus. He closes the door, puts the bus in gear and we begin again. The driver cannot see the wolf because it's hidden by the seat ahead, lying down.

I look at the bus driver. I look at the wolf. I am wondering what will happen if I yell. I think of the possibilities. One: the bus driver ignores me because he can't see the wolf; two: the bus driver stops and the wolf eats my throat. I quit there. I mean, what's the point?

Then the thought occurs to me.

What is this wolf doing here?

I look at the wolf again. He actually seems relaxed. Smiling. But his two yellow eyes are fixed on me like bayonets. He closes one of them, then opens it. Is that a wink? Do wolves wink? Do wolves get on buses, sit down next to people and wink at them? Not as far as I know. So why is he here? Is it like those whales you hear about crashing into beaches? Or moose wandering into grocery stores? Or like people going to the moon?

We are coming to my stop. Suddenly I don't care any more. I reach up and ring the bell. The wolf watches. He closes his mouth. I've called his bluff. It's his move next.

The bus pulls into the curb. I get up and walk to the rear door. The wolf gets up and follows. I look in that round mirror above the door to see the face of the driver. His mouth is wide open. The wolf and I step off the bus and into the night. The wolf grabs my left arm. He's not going to chew it off. He's taking me somewhere.

When we get far enough out of town, the wolf lets go of my arm. He walks in front of me. He doesn't bother looking back. My leather jacket keeps out the wind, but not the cold. I start wishing I had a coat like a wolf's. My ears and face are numb.

I think of this western movie I saw once. It's about this bad guy chasing a good guy in the middle of a snow storm. And the good guy finds a cave to stay in, leaving the bad guy outside. But the bad guy shoots a buffalo and cuts off his hide to wrap himself in it.

The next morning, the good guy comes out of the cave and finds the bad guy frozen stiff, wrapped in the buffalo skin which is also frozen stiff. The bad guy's gun is still pointing at the cave. The good guy breaks the gun from his frozen hand.

I am wondering what I would look like wrapped in a frozen wolf hide, found dead on some farmer's field next spring, with my knife frozen in my hand.

I suddenly realize the direction we are headed. We are going across the train bridge.

We are heading towards the Power Plant.

It's like some inner fire instantly heats up and the cold burns off. When we cross the bridge, I jog through the shallow snow and follow the wolf. We pass the dump. We pass where the old man's shack used to be. There's nothing there.

In twenty minutes I can see the orange glow of the Plant's lights. The wolf has run to the top of a hill and is outlined against the sky next to a small thicket of woods. He stops. He is waiting for me to catch up. Just before I do, he enters the thicket.

When I get to the hill top, I can see the Plant in the valley below, its stacks and buildings spread like a mouthful of broken glass. I go into the thicket where the wolf has disappeared. It is darker and the snow is deeper. I hear the growl, or rather, feel it again. I freeze.

In front of me is a small clearing. In it are four or five dark shapes. They move, quietly. They are animals of some sort. I step closer and crouch. They are deer. Four of them have surrounded a fifth. Two are facing outward and two are facing in. The one in the middle is doing something. There are sounds, the sounds of breathing hard. The one in the middle has spread its hind legs and lowers itself. Suddenly, a black bundle drops to the snowy ground.

The deer has given birth.

The mother turns and immediately starts to sniff her offspring, grabbing at it with her mouth. Suddenly, she backs away. She backs away, and leaves. The other deer sniff the bundle and follow, leaving it alone on the ground. Moving, writhing.

The wolf appears from nowhere, sniffs the writhing mass, then walks a few feet away and sits. The wolf looks at me, its yellow eyes piercing the dark.

It is my turn.

I go to the bundle. Up close I can see that it is a baby deer, struggling to get out of its filmy sack. Another bloody sack lies near the deer. The cord is still attached. I take out my knife and cut the cord. I clean off the film as best I can. I pick up the baby deer. Something is wrong.

It has no legs. There are four little stubs where the legs should be.

Something in me rips and I start crying like I've never cried before. I pick up the little deer and start walking. I know if I leave it, that it will be dead in hours. That the magpies will pick its flesh clean. I carry it back to the train bridge.

When I get to the middle of the bridge, I can feel it is still alive and moving. I hold it close to me and kiss it. Then I throw it into the night. I hear a splash in the dark waters below.

I stand there a long time. I think about jumping. I think of all the stupid things I've done. I think of the old guy. And the wolf.

I hear a train coming. It is approaching from the direction of my parent's house. I head the other way.

Acknowledgements

It is truly strange how these things come to pass. In their own ways all these people have had significant input into this collection. I would like to thank Paddy O'Rourke for suggesting I write such a thing, Seán Virgo for recognizing this voice, Scott Miller for his first look and invaluable advice, Joe Welsh for permission to tell a version of the wolf story in "Cut", Ruth Smillie for giving me a unique perspective in dealing with young voices at the Native Survival School (lo those many years ago), Jack Walton for contributing to the original idea of "The Rink", Zoey MacIntyre for keeping me honest, the Saskatchewan Writer's Guild for allowing me the time to finish this during my residency in Estevan, and all those young people who let me try these stories out on them in readings around the province of Saskatchewan.

"The Rink" first appeared in *The Blue Jean Collection* (Thistledown Press Ltd., 1992) and has been awarded the Vicky Metcalf award for short fiction.